## "I couldn't h[elp it]. [You're] so beautiful wh[en you're mad.]"

She rolled her eyes toward the ceiling and shook her head. "Words a woman longs to hear. Now…since I don't want to talk business with you unless you're here to buy yarn, I suggest you leave before you make me truly angry and find out how utterly gorgeous I can be."

Even though he knew it would probably blow up in his face, he couldn't help the grin that formed. "I like you, Lilly Barnes. I hope you'll let me look at your basement and then listen to my offer."

"Bribery, huh? I have to say you've caught my attention."

"I prefer to think of it as incentive."

She nodded toward a door at the back of the shop. "It couldn't hurt to let you look."

One small victory. He tried not to irritate her with a smile.

## Books by Missy Tippens

Love Inspired

*Her Unlikely Family*
*His Forever Love*
*A Forever Christmas*
*A Family for Faith*
*A House Full of Hope*
*Georgia Sweethearts*

## MISSY TIPPENS

Born and raised in Kentucky, Missy met her very own hero when she headed to grad school in Atlanta, Georgia. She promptly fell in love and hasn't left Georgia since. She and her pastor husband have been married twenty-five-plus years now and have been blessed with three wonderful children and an assortment of pets.

Missy is thankful to God that she's been called to write stories of love and faith. After ten years of pursuing her dream of being published, she made her first sale of a full-length novel to the Love Inspired line. She still pinches herself to see if it really happened!

Missy would love to hear from readers through her website, www.missytippens.com, or by email at missytippens@aol.com. For those with no internet access, you may reach her c/o Love Inspired Books, 233 Broadway, Suite 1001, New York, NY 10279.

# Georgia Sweethearts
## Missy Tippens

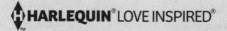
HARLEQUIN® LOVE INSPIRED®

Recycling programs
for this product may
not exist in your area.

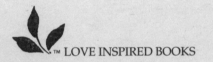 ™ LOVE INSPIRED BOOKS

ISBN-13: 978-0-373-81686-6

GEORGIA SWEETHEARTS

Copyright © 2013 by Melissa L. Tippens

www.LoveInspiredBooks.com

**Printed in U.S.A.**

And now these three remain: faith, hope and love.
But the greatest of these is love.
—*1 Corinthians* 13:13

Trust in the Lord with all your heart and lean not
on your own understanding; in all your ways submit
to him, and he will make your paths straight.
—*Proverbs* 3:5,6

To my agent Natasha Kern—
For your unfailing encouragement.

To my readers—
For letters and emails that touch my heart.

To God—
For the lessons
You teach me through the journey of each book.

## Acknowledgments

Thanks to author Shirley Jump for her online
writing classes and for invaluable feedback on my
homework assignments—which became this story!

Special thanks to Gail White
for generously sharing her time and talent
by starting the Yarners group at my church. And
to Marla Weaver and Penny for patiently teaching
this hopeless knitter how to attempt to make a scarf.
Maybe someday I'll finish it.

Thank you to my amazing editors Emily Rodmell
and Elizabeth Mazer for your guidance
and for making the book better.
I'm blessed to be able to work with you.

A big thank-you to all the other wonderful folks
at Love Inspired Books, especially those who
do the behind-the-scenes work.
Please know that I appreciate you!

## Chapter One

The third time Lillianne Barnes dropped the knitting needle—along with two stitches—should have been a clue. But she kept clacking the needles and wrapping the yarn like Great-Aunt Talitha had taught her, trying to make the soft blue yarn into something...*anything*. She glanced at the supposedly simple, "no-fail" directions. No fail for everyone else, maybe. But not for her.

Lilly chewed her lip as she tried one more time to carefully slip the loop of yarn to complete the transfer of the stitch from one needle to the other. It went where it was supposed to go, but the last two uneven loops followed prematurely and began to unravel.

She'd left her perfectly good job as manager of women's clothing at a high-end department store—secure, enjoyable, with benefits—for this...mess?

With a growl, she tossed the whole bundle aside. "I give up. I *cannot* knit."

"Must be a problem if you work in a yarn shop."

She yelped, then jumped up, the metal folding chair scraping the floor behind her. A man built like a professional athlete stood in the doorway watching her with a bemused expression. His dark blond hair, playful blue eyes and crooked smile made her suck in a breath and hold it. Still, gorgeous or not, Mr. Six-Foot-Plus and his big, broad shoulders *had* barged in, ignoring the sign out front.

She exhaled long and loud, as if she found his presence annoying, though in reality, she was more frustrated by her clash with the knitting needles than by the handsome intruder. "I'm sorry, we're closed for the day."

He held up his hands palms forward. "I apologize for scaring you. I'm not here to buy anything." He stepped farther into the room, his rugged jacket and muscular build out of place next to the softest of baby yarns. "My name is Daniel Foreman. I'm Ann Sealy's grandson."

Ann, Aunt Talitha's good friend. The ache of loss once again settled in Lilly's chest, squeezing like a fist.

Lilly left the circle of folding chairs in the corner and walked behind the counter, trying to remember if she'd seen this man at the funeral. But that whole week was still a blur.

She busied her hands straightening receipts, anything to keep from giving in to the tears stinging her eyes. "Your grandmother was very kind to help my great-aunt in her last days."

"I've met Jenna. So you must be Lilly, the other niece who inherited this place." His friendly expression gentled as he moved to the counter. "I'm sorry for your loss. Miss Talitha was a kind, generous woman."

"Thank you." A fresh wave of grief battered her already-tender heart. Talitha Barnes *had* been both kind and generous. But more than that, she'd been the only family Lilly and her sister, Jenna, could ever count on. Their aunt's long-distance love had been the one constant throughout their unstable childhood.

"I heard you lived in Louisville before moving here to Georgia. Has coming to as small a town as Corinthia been a shock?"

"A bit. But everyone's been really nice."

"So how's business?"

"A little slow today." And the day before. And the day before that. At his look of sympathy, she escaped to the corner seating area and picked up her knitting, pulling out the remaining stitches and starting over.

She wouldn't share the fact that The Yarn Barn was in terrible financial shape. That she'd only sold three measly skeins of yarn earlier that day—from the bargain bin.

Or that Aunt Talitha had requested Lilly and Jenna run the store one full year before selling the business.

Once again, her heart raced—this time in anxiety—making her face tingle and her hands go numb. Not helpful when working with pointy needles.

"So you don't knit, huh?" The sparkle returned to his eyes, teasing her, pushing away his look of sympathy...and with it, a little of her grief and panic.

As she fought for slow, even breaths, she glanced at the bins full of colorful yarn, at the shiny new computer on the sales counter, at the rack of pattern books—anywhere but in his eyes. Then she forced herself to meet his smile with her own. "Can't knit. Or crochet. I'm a total klutz when it comes to anything craft-oriented."

A laugh burst out of him, deep and rumbling, warming her, tempting her to relax, to quit worrying so much.

This time, she couldn't look away from those playful blue eyes. She joined in the laughter. "Ironic, huh? Please don't advertise my ineptitude."

"I guess it wouldn't be good for business."

As their gazes locked and held, something passed between them. A kind of connection, or attraction.

She shook off the ridiculous notion. A good-looking man comes in, and she acts like an idiot, imagining things.

She stuffed her ugly, uneven knitting into the canvas tote bag to practice that night at home—Jenna's home—and concentrated on the positive. Another day passed. One day closer to fulfilling the stipulation of her aunt's will.

He turned and stared toward the back wall where she'd displayed some of her photos. "Nice. Who took these?"

"They're mine. I majored in photojournalism. Ended up in retail." When she returned to Kentucky, she planned to remedy that. To finally risk trying the career she'd always wanted.

"Sounds like an interesting story." He moved closer to inspect one—her favorite, of an elderly woman in Appalachia looking up from a quilt she was working on, laughing. A woman who'd reminded Lilly of Aunt Talitha.

He tilted his head a little to the left. Then he took a step back but kept examining the photo. "You really captured the spirit of the woman in this one."

She swallowed, touched that he'd shown interest. "Thanks."

For a few seconds, he glanced away as if embarrassed. But then, squaring his shoulders, he said, "So is this a place for knitters to hang out?" He sat in one of six rickety folding chairs, dwarfing it, as he checked out the room.

Expecting the chair to buckle at any moment, she watched his expression fall into a slight frown as he inspected the hinges on the chair. She agreed with the sad state of some of the equipment, but they didn't have the money to do anything about it. "What can I help you with, Daniel?"

He quit his perusal and stood. "I'm sorry to bother you after hours. But I've come by to check on the agreement to rent the basement of your building."

Rent downstairs? "What agreement?"

His brows drew downward. "Didn't Talitha mention she'd agreed to let our church rent the space?"

What had her aunt been thinking? "Well, actually...no. Please fill me in."

"I'm pastor of a fairly new church, and we've outgrown our meeting space."

"A pastor?" The man certainly didn't look like he spent his day behind a desk. Or a pulpit.

He confirmed it with a nod. "In her last weeks, Talitha wasn't doing well, and the shop was struggling. So my grandmother suggested she rent us the basement as a solution for everyone."

"Aunt Talitha agreed?"

"She did. Told me we could have the space if we wanted it. I was hoping to take a look around. If it's suitable, we're ready to move in."

"We can't finish the basement right now. Plus, when we do, I plan to offer classes." In the unlikely event she mastered knitting. "I'll need the space."

The pleasant look he'd maintained since entering the shop gave way to a flicker of impatience. But then he masked it. "If our church grows quickly enough, we wouldn't be in your way for long. I don't have anything in writing, but I hope you'll consider honoring Talitha's verbal offer." He pulled a business card out of his pocket and gave it to her. "Give me a call any time." He backed away and waved, once again the epitome of charm. "I'll let you get back to your, uh, knitting?"

*Ha-ha.* He thought he was so funny. She narrowed

her eyes at him. "I'll have you know, I *used* to know how." No need to admit she'd never been more than proficient.

His crooked smile morphed into a full-fledged grin that sent her heart rate off the charts. A grin she'd find seriously attractive, if it weren't coupled with the fact he was proving to be a complication to her plans for boosting business at the shop, a complication who seemed to think he was a comedian, no less.

"My apologies for underestimating your talent." The teasing look in his eyes said otherwise. "I look forward to seeing your needlework, Lilly. Soon." He gave a jaunty salute as he turned and left the shop.

She tried to suck in a full, stuttering breath to tell him he didn't need to bother coming back. But of course, he'd already shut the door behind him.

She thought about his joke and had to laugh. She'd be a fool to let him get under her skin just because he was so attractive and they'd shared a moment. Besides, it wasn't Daniel's fault she was inept at all things crafty. It wasn't his fault the store was struggling.

And even though she'd like to blame him, it wasn't his fault she found it difficult to resist his charm.

No, she needed to look into his claim. What if Aunt Talitha *had* made the promise?

The thought sent her heart to racing once again. She'd recently moved to town. Had just joined Jenna in running the business. At the moment, income wasn't keeping pace with outgo. And they still hadn't been able to reach the shop's accountant to learn more about the financials. Now they might have to add landlord duties, as well?

They knew nothing about leasing property. And they'd first have to finish off the basement, which they couldn't afford.

She wished she could simply claim *new owner, new policies*. Especially since he and Talitha hadn't put anything in writing. But her conscience said she needed to investigate further. Just one more thing to add to the mile-long list of tasks for the business.

She couldn't bear to see her aunt's beloved shop fail. It was the least she could do for the only family member to show her and Jenna love. She looked around the room at the diverse colors and textures. Bins of soft acrylics, rougher wools, knobby blends. All strange and new to her. New like her life in this small Georgia town that Aunt Talitha had loved. Lilly had a promise to fulfill.

Now, back to the first item on the list. To make a go of it, she did need to learn—*relearn*—to knit and crochet. A huge sigh escaped as she picked up her tote bag of yarn to practice that night. With her skill level, she wasn't worthy of the luxurious fluff of sky-blue yarn.

Blue the exact shade of Daniel's eyes.

She pushed away the thought like a pesky fly. She would love to avoid Daniel at all costs.

But the stack of bills behind the counter reminded

her that she better find a way to make the shop profitable—and soon. Or else, agreement or not, she'd be forced to accept his offer.

Daniel chuckled as he reflected on the meeting. With cheeks flushing, her chin raised high, Lilly Barnes had proven she was a spitfire. Had scorched him with one flash of those big hazel eyes. Eyes that had warned him away.

His laughter died on his lips. So why had he felt that pull between them? Even after her clear hesitation over the idea of renting to them, he'd felt the sizzle of attraction. Had enjoyed the good-natured banter about her knitting.

He had to remember she was still grieving. He shouldn't force the issue, but he would have to figure out a way to convince Lilly to rent to him. They didn't have any other affordable leads.

When he pulled in his grandmother's driveway and saw his dad's car, he glanced at the clock on the dash. Why did his father have to be here the one night he'd come in late?

Determined to hold his tongue throughout dinner, he hurried up the driveway and around to the back.

Light from the kitchen spilled out onto the back porch, soothing some of Daniel's tension. He loved this place. Had spent a lot of summers here after his mother had died, after his dad had further buried himself in work. Though his dad had tried to ease the burden on family members by shipping Daniel from relative to relative, time with GranAnn had been his favorite.

Ever since, the white clapboard house with the homey kitchen had been a haven. When she'd asked him to live with her while he started the church in Corinthia, he'd jumped at the chance.

He stepped inside the kitchen door, the aroma of freshly baked bread like a hug from the woman herself.

"Oh, good. I'm glad you made it, baby." Gran's light blue eyes lacked their usual spark, and her normally easy smile seemed strained, as if begging him to behave and play nice. She patted his back and directed his attention toward the table. "Look who's joined us." Once again, GranAnn was trying to force them to spend time together. Something Daniel had tried to do in the past and had failed.

Blake Foreman, a carbon copy of Daniel except for his graying temples and faint wrinkles, sat straight as a goalpost, looking down his disapproving nose. "You're late."

"I apologize," Daniel forced out.

Semiretired, Blake had moved to Corinthia a couple months before Daniel. "Seems you could have called to let your grandmother know you were delayed." Blue eyes a shade deeper than Daniel's narrowed, issuing a challenge.

Anytime the two of them got together, they were like two dogs circling each other, readying for a fight. Animosity sizzled in the air, something he wanted to reach out and seize, to try to understand. But tonight he didn't have the energy for the struggle.

He pulled away his attention from his dad. "I'm sorry I didn't make it earlier, GranAnn. I had a late counseling session, then got delayed over at the yarn shop with Lilly Barnes."

"Oh, good, I'm glad you two met." With a relieved, happy grin, she motioned for him to sit. "I kept your plate warm."

Only then did he notice they'd already finished eating. Man, when he messed up, he messed up good.

GranAnn bustled around the kitchen with her familiar floral apron around her waist, pouring syrupy sweet iced tea from the same brown glass pitcher she'd had when he was child.

Blake leaned back and crossed his arms. "Who's this Lilly Barnes?"

Daniel was tempted to tell him it was none of his concern. Instead, he opted to break down and ask for help.

*As if he would ever get involved in something important to me.*

He swallowed back his bitterness. The church had to come first. "Lilly and her sister, Jenna, inherited the yarn shop at the edge of town. The former owner had agreed to rent the basement to our church since we need a bigger space. Apparently Lilly knew nothing about the arrangement."

"Oh, it's the perfect space," GranAnn added. "I'm sure Lilly and Jenna will be glad to rent it to you." She pulled his plate out of the oven with a dish towel to keep from burning herself and set the meat loaf and mashed potatoes on the place mat in front of him.

Daniel put the faded cloth napkin in his lap. "Since we've been drawing more people from over in Appleton, the location is perfect. I just haven't seen the basement yet to confirm it's large enough to hold at least fifty. Lilly didn't seem willing to show me around."

"So she's not going to honor the previous owner's contract?" Blake asked.

"We don't have anything in writing, and I didn't want to force the issue. She's still grieving the loss of her great-aunt. Do you know of any other place that would hold fifty—within our small budget?"

"No," Gran said, clutching his arm, her face pinched in a grimace of worry. "Promise me you won't give up. Those girls need the rent money, even if they're not willing to admit it yet. You have to help them."

He couldn't remember ever seeing his grandmother so tense. "Since we've outgrown our current location, I have to put the church first. But I plan to talk to her again."

His grandmother relaxed into her chair with a huff. As if she'd accomplished something that left her drained. "Blake, Daniel's done a wonderful job with the church. Especially getting his members involved ministering to the community." She squeezed Daniel's hand in her warm, soft grasp as she stared into his eyes, pride beaming. "You should be proud of your son."

Daniel smiled his appreciation even as he girded himself for his father's dismissal.

"Fifty, huh?" Blake asked.

For a split second, he thought his dad looked surprised—maybe even pleased—at the rapid growth. Then he realized Blake probably found the size laughable. Disappointed by his son's career change, he'd probably be happy if Daniel's venture failed.

"We're nearing fifty," Daniel said. "I'd like to have room for growth until we find a permanent location."

"Doesn't matter to me what size. You quit a lucrative job against my advice. Then poured good money into seminary, only to recklessly start your own church instead of taking a position at an established one with a dependable income."

He'd heard the same spiel from his dad so many times he could recite it word for word. The man acted as if Daniel had taken up a life of crime.

"So do you know of anywhere we could rent?" Daniel asked, unable to keep the exasperation from his voice.

"Nope." Blake pushed away from the table. "Ann, I'm sorry, but I need to go. I'm expecting a conference call."

Her eyes flashed as she got up from the table. Nothing made her madder than family members who didn't get along. "I hope you can stay longer next time. Maybe schedule that call for earlier in the day."

She opened the refrigerator and hunkered in front of the shelves as if searching for something, no doubt avoiding further confrontation with her son-in-law. Daniel could imagine her clenching her jaw to keep from speaking her mind. He understood the temptation.

"Thank you for an excellent dinner." With nothing more than a nod of the head at Daniel, Blake exited the back door, shutting it quietly behind him, as if to prove he was the only one in control of his emotions.

GranAnn popped out of the refrigerator and smacked the door shut. "If I didn't love that man like my own son, I'd have to shake him 'til his teeth rattled."

At the image of his tiny grandmother shaking his brawny father, Daniel laughed. "I'd be happy to help."

"Don't you give up on your daddy. He's bottled up a lot of pain. I think having you both here in Corinthia is a blessing. God can work miracles."

Yeah, he'd started praying for that miracle at the age of nine, when he realized other boys had dads who didn't work every waking hour, dads who showed up for peewee football games, who ate meals at home and tucked their kids into bed at night. He'd prayed for a dad who cared until the day he left for college, when he finally let go of the desire to matter to his father and changed his focus to look to the future. To quit wallowing in self-pity and make a difference in the world.

"You must be starving. Now eat," Gran said.

He bowed his head and thanked God for the food.

As soon as he opened his eyes, she dropped into the chair across from him. "Cricket's mother called before dinner. She wanted to thank you for coming over this afternoon. Said she thought Cricket seemed better."

The breath rushed out of him in a surge of relief. The girl, pregnant at fifteen, was severely depressed. "Good news. I'm meeting with the family again next week."

"Even better news is Cricket has finally agreed to see a psychiatrist about the depression."

"I'm glad. I should probably follow up with her parents, to make sure she goes. I'm uncomfortable waiting a week before we meet again."

A sense of unease over Cricket wouldn't let up. He decided to call her mom in the morning to offer assistance. Then, he'd regroup and figure out a way to convince Lilly Barnes that renting out her basement could benefit them both.

Lilly walked in the front door of her sister and brother-in-law's house, her temporary home, tension knotting her gut over what she'd find inside. As if concern over the yarn shop hadn't already tied her stomach tightly enough.

"I'm home," she called. Both Jenna's and Ned's vehicles were there. Which meant potential for an evening of arguing.

The cool, dark entry hall enveloped her. Quiet. A good sign. Maybe she'd dreaded coming inside for no reason. Maybe tonight would be one of the good nights.

As she hung up her coat in the closet, her stomach started to relax. Then a bedroom door slammed down the hallway of the tiny two-bedroom rental. Behind the closed door, voices raised, one high-pitched, the other low.

Jenna and Ned.

She considered slipping out to go to a restaurant, but then a whimper came from the family room.

*Will.*

She headed toward the sound and found her ten-month-old nephew standing in the exercise saucer, leaning over, trying to reach a toy on the floor.

"Hey, sweet thing. Did you drop your doggie?"

Will's big brown eyes lit up, and he gave her a slobbery grin that made her feel like the most important person in the world. He sprang up and down on his chunky little legs as he raised his arms to her, straining for all he was worth.

She pulled him up and out of his seat and kissed the top of his head, the silky brown curls tickling her nose, the powdery scent of baby shampoo calming her. Then she handed him his toy. "Let's go see what's for dinner."

The voices down the hall escalated, but Will didn't flinch. Apparently, he'd grown accustomed to his parents arguing. Like she and Jenna had grown accustomed to *their* parents arguing. Or so she'd told herself.

Lilly blew out a huge sigh as she headed toward the kitchen, wishing that she could as easily exhale all the old memories and be rid of them permanently.

Jenna pretended all was well in the Jones household, but Lilly knew better. And from what she'd observed, she feared Jenna and Ned might not be able to work out their differences. Jenna refused to go to marriage counseling. Why couldn't she see she'd snagged a decent guy worth fighting for? He was a good father, a hardworking firefighter who loved Jenna. If not for Ned's help, they couldn't have managed repairing the yarn shop building.

Yet, Jenna seemed to have checked out, sabotaging the relationship, just like she had every other one. Lilly hoped Ned would be patient and not give up on his wife.

Though the tiny kitchen's countertop was stacked with a day's worth of dirty dishes, Jenna had left a pot of chili simmering on the stovetop. Two jars of unopened baby food sat on the high chair tray beside a clean bib. "Looks like you and me, kid. Dinner for two. Although I'll pass on your smooshed-up peas."

She placed him in his chair and snapped the bib

in place. The spicy steam wafted her way, making her stomach growl, but she needed to feed Will first.

As she opened the jars of food, he banged the tray and started to fuss. "Eee!" His impatient version of *eat*.

He cranked up a pitiful wail. A splash of Cheerios on his tray appeased his appetite and allowed for independence as his little fingers snagged the oat circles he loved. Since he usually spit out half of what she fed him, she'd learned to distract him with the cereal while she tried to sneak in some vegetables and meat.

They'd managed some success with her method when she heard Ned's heavy footsteps coming down the hall toward the kitchen.

He walked in, cheeks high in color, dark, wavy hair disheveled. "Hi, Lilly." He kissed his son on the head. Wiped a smear of sweet potatoes off Will's cheek. "Eat like a good boy. Daddy's got to go to work."

She couldn't ignore the elephant in the room. "Ned, I'd be glad to move out if it would help. I don't want my presence to cause additional strain for you two."

His cheeks flushed redder. His dark brown eyes darted around the room as if he was embarrassed by her comment. "No. Stay. You're good for her, and for Will, too. It's just…" He ruffled Will's hair as his throat bobbed up, then down. "I'll see y'all later."

Her appetite followed him right out the door.

Jenna walked in the kitchen shortly after, her pretty green eyes red and swollen. She wore sweatpants and a faded, holey college T-shirt. "Thanks for feeding Will," she said as she grabbed a bowl and ladled out a small portion of chili. Enough for a mouse.

"You need to eat more."

"I can't."

"What'd y'all argue about this time?"

"Nothing."

"That *nothing* made you cry."

Jenna plopped the bowl onto the scratched pressed-wood table and slid into her chair. She'd forgotten a spoon but didn't seem to notice. Lilly got up to get one, waiting for her to talk.

"Thanks," she said, taking the spoon, then proceeding to shove the chili around the bowl, never taking a single bite.

"I'll feed you, too, if I have to."

That drew a little smile. "We can't agree on anything. He wants to spend. I want to save. He wants to buy a house. I want to rent a little longer. He wants to go to church on Sundays. I want to stay home and have family time. He wants another baby. I don't."

Lilly wasn't a professional therapist, but she understood that with her and Jenna's family history, trust was an issue. Jenna's actions all pointed to someone who was afraid to believe her relationship had a future. "Sounds like maybe you should go with him to talk to a marriage counselor."

"That's not going to help at this point." She nibbled a tiny bite, enough to nourish a flea. "Let's talk about something else."

Will banged on the high chair and squealed, ready to get up and move again. They'd somehow managed to get most of the two jars of food into his stomach with only a small percentage landing on his bib and in his hair. Success, in Lilly's opinion.

Jenna got to her feet to reach for Will, but Lilly pushed her sister back into her chair. "I'll get him. You need to eat or you won't do him any good."

As Lilly stood at the kitchen sink waiting for the water to warm to wipe Will's hands and face, Jenna withdrew into her own world.

Time to distract her from her thoughts. "I had a visitor to the shop today. Daniel Foreman, Ann's grandson."

"Hmm?"

"Daniel Foreman. He came to the shop today."

Jenna turned toward Lilly, her eyes refocusing in the present. "Oh, he's the pastor who started the new church. What'd he want?"

"He claims Aunt Talitha agreed to rent out the basement as a meeting space for the church." She reached for Will's hands to wipe them before he latched onto her hair. "Did you know anything about it?"

"No." Jenna propped her elbow on the table and rested her chin in her palm. She looked totally forlorn. "That's the church Ned's been attending, wanting me to visit. I can't say I'd relish having them around. They already tie up too much of his time."

So much for taking her mind off her marital problems. "I don't see how they could rent it until we finish the space, and we can't afford that right now."

"They'd be there all the time—apparently they're pretty active with the community service projects all week long. Ned's mentioned some kind of afterschool mentoring program. He's volunteering with a food pantry and a clothes closet ministry." She rolled her eyes. "Reminded me of that old busybody neighbor we had, Mrs. What's-Her-Name, who brought us clothes and reported Mom and Dad to the social worker."

Humiliation nearly two-decades old stung Lilly's face as if the act had happened yesterday. Mrs. Wiley had come from across the street with a bag of new dollar-store shorts and tops and, within viewing and hearing range of other neighbor kids, wrinkled her nose in disgust and offered to wash Lilly and Jenna's clothing for them since their parents didn't seem to care.

Even if the woman's intentions had been good, she'd carried out the act of charity in a scarring manner. And set their dad on course to uproot and move his family once again, tearing them away from some good people of a local church who had been quietly helping her and Jenna—people who'd shown them kindness and love.

Old anger burned like acid in Lilly's stomach. "I've done some figuring. If we hold a few small knitting classes upstairs, we'll generate income from fees and selling the supplies. We should be able to get by until we can afford to renovate the basement to hold larger classes."

"Who'd teach?"

Lilly eyed her sister for evidence she was poking fun, and immediately thought of Daniel, teasing, promising to come back to see her knitting. She ignored the warm, cozy feeling and checked her sister's face. Not a hint of a smile. "I don't know. But I'll work on it. In the meantime, I'm going to check Aunt Talitha's records for any information on the agreement with Daniel."

Jenna pushed away her barely touched bowl and wiped her mouth. "You know, that rent money would be a sure thing."

"Yeah, but we'd have to spend a lot to get there. Besides, building a sense of community is important for our type of business. I'd rather ask Ned to help us get started on finishing the basement, to create a place for customers to hang out. That way, there's no deadline and no rush. Volunteer labor, of course, until we can afford—"

"He's gone."

A frisson of alarm passed over her. Surely Jenna

didn't mean that in the way it sounded. Surely he'd just left for work. "What do you mean, *gone?*"

Jenna looked up, her pain-filled eyes welling with tears. "Ned can't help us with the store anymore. He left me."

# Chapter Two

Armed with two lists, Daniel headed to The Yarn Barn the next day, trying to keep his promise to his grandmother. He hoped to at least get a peek at the basement to see if it was as ideal a setting as Gran had asserted. Though he wouldn't push Lilly and her sister, he did need to find the church a new location soon.

His first list included all the advantages of allowing the church to rent—including the idea for the church to renovate the space—as well as the perks they would offer.

The second list was extra incentive. An evaluation of her store's current visibility in the community, along with suggestions to increase exposure. Might as well use his marketing expertise to help.

He pulled into the gravel parking lot and got a good look at the place in daylight. Granted, the building was old. But the structure, painted barn red, with a sloping roof and white trim, had charm. Was quaint and welcoming.

Wind chimes jingled as he walked in, something new she'd added since his visit yesterday.

"May I help   Oh. Daniel," she said, voice flat. Disappointed. She may as well have said, *oh, it's just you.*

He considered her attitude a challenge.

"Hello, Lilly." For the first time, he noticed one whole wall lined with cubbyholes packed with yarn of every color. "The store's certainly well stocked."

"Our aunt's inventory was depleted when we came on board. We had to place a large order of supplies." Her sad gaze darted away as she ran her hand over a closed laptop computer, wiping away invisible dust. "Can I help you find something? A gift for your grandmother, maybe?"

If a sale would put him in her good graces... "Uh, sure. Do you have a nice scarf?"

Pushing long, dark hair behind one ear, she winced. "I'm afraid I don't have many finished items left. A couple hats. A pair of children's mittens." Her expression brightened as she came from behind the counter. "I remember Aunt Talitha talking about Ann knitting. Maybe I can interest you in some yarn. Along with a new pattern book?"

The hopeful look in her eyes smacked him in the gut. "I need to come clean. I didn't really come in to buy a gift. I stopped by to talk business."

Her eyes shot sparks as they focused all her ire on him. "Thank goodness you're *honest,* Reverend."

Her sarcasm wasn't lost on him. Though he deserved the censure, he had to battle a smile. With her big greenish-brown eyes and rosy cheeks, she had to be the prettiest angry woman he'd ever seen. "I'm sorry."

"You don't look sorry."

"I'm sorry. For not looking sorry, that is." A chuckle rumbled out before he could stop it. When she glared harder, he added, "Sorry."

Before she could say anything else, he held up a hand. "I couldn't help it. You're just so beautiful when you're mad."

She rolled her eyes toward the ceiling and shook her head. "Words a woman longs to hear. Now… since I don't want to talk business with you unless you're here to buy yarn, I suggest you leave before you make me truly angry and find out how utterly gorgeous I can be."

Even though he knew it would probably blow up in his face, he couldn't help the grin that formed. "I like you, Lilly Barnes. I hope you'll let me look at your basement and then listen to my offer."

She crossed her arms but didn't throw him out.

"We would pay rent, of course," he said quickly. "And to sweeten the deal, we'd do any work you need to finish the basement, deducting the cost of materials out of the rent. Labor would be donated by church members, the teenagers I'm mentoring… and me."

Something akin to interest flashed across her face.

He held up the paper with his first list. "The names of five women in my congregation who knit or crochet. Two said they'd be willing to teach you. My grandmother might even be persuaded to teach a class for you if you give her a call. She taught for Talitha when she opened the shop."

"Bribery, huh? I have to say, you've caught my attention."

"I prefer to think of it as incentive." Incentive to follow through with her aunt's promise.

She nodded toward a door at the back of the shop. "It couldn't hurt to let you look."

One small victory. He tried not to irritate her with a smile.

She led the way down a set of steps into a cool, damp space. Definitely needed dehumidifiers. But it was a nice large space that would easily hold some tables and fifty chairs. The walls were finished, but they'd need to paint and put in a drop ceiling. Add more lighting. Maybe build a small room for an office that she could later convert to a storage closet.

A plan began to take shape. He couldn't imagine her wanting to deal with the renovation on her own. "It wouldn't be too difficult to make the basement functional."

"Looks dreary to me," she said. "Lots of work to make it livable."

He squatted down to check for moisture on a crack in the cement floor. "I've been on several mission trips. This is a piece of cake compared to what I've worked on."

"We still plan to hold classes down here at some point. I wouldn't want the space tied up indefinitely." She rubbed her hands up and down her arms as if trying to warm herself.

With the winter cold outside, he'd have to beef up the heating system, as well. "If 'indefinitely' is the problem, we can put an end date on the contract. And maybe work out a way to share the space so you can hold classes if you're ready sooner than expected."

Surely, he'd tempted her with his offer.

She looked around the room, her hazel eyes more brown than green in the dim lighting. Dark, mysterious eyes…beautiful. Beauty wasn't what drew him to her, though. He'd like to get to know her better and, since they'd gotten off on the wrong foot, to make her change her mind about him.

She shivered. "This business ownership is all very new. I'm still looking at my aunt's records, figuring out the financials. I'd like time to look through her paperwork to see if she mentioned the agreement."

"Let's go upstairs. It's too cold to talk down here."

When they got to the heated area, she rubbed her hands together and the tension eased out of her shoulders.

The warmth made him relax, as well. Though the

seating area was small and had those rickety folding chairs, she'd done a nice job making it as homey and comfortable as possible. That, and the rainbow of colors from the wall of yarn, made it a place customers would enjoy spending time. And money.

Should he bring up his second list, his suggestions for marketing?

She shivered again. "Ooh. Goodness."

"Having trouble getting rid of the damp chill?" He pulled off his jacket and placed it around her shoulders. "There. Maybe that'll help."

Before he knew it, he was lost in her eyes. He could hardly breathe as she stared back at him.

Confusion clouded her expression, then she looked away…and retreated behind the sales counter. The solid wood structure served as a firm boundary, Lilly wielding it like a shield.

She smiled. An impersonal, dismissive thing. For some reason, he wanted to make her smile for real. Like the first day they met, before he started talking business.

"Well, Daniel, you've seen the basement now. Are you sure you still want to lease it?"

"It'll fit our needs nicely."

"You've made a generous offer. I'll need to discuss it with Jenna. And I don't want to make any decisions until I meet with Aunt Talitha's accountant tomorrow. Is there anything else you need today?"

"Would you go to dinner with me?" Heat blasted

from his neck up to his face. Had he really said that out loud?

The shocked look on her face confirmed it.

"To discuss some ideas I've had," he added quickly. "About marketing your shop. It's what I do...did." He snapped his mouth shut before he embarrassed himself further.

"I'm sorry, but I can't." She flipped her hair over her shoulder. Gloriously wavy, brown hair that trailed halfway down her back. "Thank you, though. It's that...well...life's a little hectic right now..."

He'd flustered her. Probably messed up everything. He had to do damage control, and quick. "How about coming to our service on Sunday? Meet some folks. I think you'll find we'd be good tenants."

If he'd thought she was tense earlier, at the mention of the church service she turned into marble. Whether she physically moved or not, he wasn't sure, but she'd definitely distanced herself. Had put up a wall.

"Um, no thank you. I help my sister with my nephew whenever I'm not working. Sunday is our day to clean the house."

Even though he sensed it wouldn't do any good, he had to try. Maybe if he took away her excuses, she'd tell him the real reason. "We have a nursery worker who watches the younger children. Bring both of them and come."

She looked all around the room as if searching for an escape route. "Look, you need to know you shouldn't waste your time preaching to me. What little childhood faith Jenna and I had got crushed out of us by our parents."

Anger burned in his gut. But he tamped it down. "Were your parents abusive?"

She glanced away. Shook her head. "I pretty much raised Jenna. We were too busy getting by to go to church regularly."

"I'm sorry." This time he really meant the words. He hated to think of her and Jenna suffering. "I hope, now that you're adults, you'll give worship a try. We have small group meetings, Bible studies and—"

A forced laugh burst out of her, as if she was trying to blow off the painful glimpse of her childhood. "Now I feel like one of your projects."

The ease with which she dismissed his concern spoke volumes. She was an expert at covering the hurt.

This wasn't the time to talk business or marketing. "Just know the invitation stands. We'd love to have you anytime. We meet at ten o'clock Sunday mornings at Frank's Pizza Place, downtown Corinthia."

"At a restaurant?"

"Yeah. Frank's a member of the congregation and offered the space. But it's a tight fit. That, and the noise in the kitchen while they prep for lunch can be distracting."

A tentative smile revealed a little dimple forming at the left corner of her mouth. She pulled her lips back over her teeth, almost self-consciously. "I imagine growling stomachs distract, as well."

"Especially mine."

When she laughed, his heart squeezed in his chest. He suddenly wished…what? That he could keep making her laugh?

She grabbed a cloth at the end of the counter and swiped it over the wooden surface, her dimple still in place. "I can't keep up with the dust."

He had no business wanting to make her laugh. He should pray for her, for God to heal her painful past. "I appreciate you showing me around. Hope to see you on Sunday."

The moment of friendliness ended as she reestablished the barrier, eyes cooling, smile tempering. "Thank you for the information on the church services."

Her insinuation? *Thanks, but no thanks.* He suspected she blamed God for her rough childhood. If so, would she ever agree to rent the space to a church?

Lilly had played phone tag for days before finally getting an appointment to meet with her great-aunt's accountant, Mr. W. R. Andrews. Afterward, as she escaped his office, she wished she hadn't bothered.

Jenna, manning the shop but leery of handling customers with a baby to watch, had asked Lilly to take Will with her to the appointment. Which hadn't made the news easier to swallow.

Working around Will's warm jacket, she strapped him in his car seat, kissed his cheek then closed herself in the front seat of the car. She shoved her hands into her hair, grabbed hold at the roots and tugged as she voiced the growling sound she'd wanted to make for the past half hour.

Will giggled as if she'd given the funniest performance ever.

Outside the confines of her vehicle, the peaceful little town of Corinthia mocked the turmoil inside her. A grand courthouse sat in the middle of the quaint downtown square, surrounded by little shops, a white-steepled church and a library. But nothing about the picturesque scene could calm her after the meeting she'd just had with Talitha's tax guy.

She turned to Will. "You're probably hungry, aren't you, sweetie? Let's go eat lunch."

"Mama."

"Mommy is working right now." And would hopefully get in the swing of retail sales with a child around. "You get to eat lunch with me today," she said with a smile, pitching her voice to reassure a tired, hungry boy who wanted his mommy. And who'd patiently sat through the appointment.

Apparently, Aunt Talitha's record keeping left a lot to be desired. Nothing had been computerized. She'd thrown receipts in large manila envelopes and just filed them away at the end of each month. Mr. Andrews, a kind, elderly man who had patted Lilly's hand and tried his best to reassure her, said that Talitha had piled everything in a box and brought it to him to deal with quarterly.

He'd then calmly informed her that he'd had to file for a tax extension while her great aunt had been sick, and that if Lilly would pile everything in a box and bring it to him, he would take care of it.

Her heart raced from thinking about it again. Lilly couldn't afford to pay him for the hours it would take to wade through hoards of receipts. She needed to get a handle on the finances herself. Pull together the sales numbers and receipts into a file and then take it to Mr. Andrews to prepare the tax forms.

She took a deep, slow breath and tried to push away the worry.

One step at a time. Her job for the afternoon was to dig through all the records and come up with a new bookkeeping system. But only after feeding Will and—

A knock on the car window made her jump.

*Daniel.* Smiling at her.

His perfectly even, white teeth and movie-star-blue eyes set her on edge. Made her want to temper her own smile to hide the fact she'd never had braces to fix the slight overlap of her two front teeth.

She fumbled for her keys so she could get power to roll down the window. She still couldn't figure him out—his good humor, his laughter, even when she hadn't exactly welcomed him.

*He's offered to do the work I can't ask Ned to do now that he's left Jenna.* She'd tried not to panic since Jenna had dropped the bomb about their separation. And now they had the additional worry over possibly having to pay an accountant for more hours than they'd anticipated.

"Sorry I startled you again," he said as the window slid slowly downward.

"I didn't see you standing there."

"Hey, buddy," he said when he spotted Will. Then he leaned down to look at her. "So what's got you tearing out your hair?"

Oh, no. He'd seen her fit of frustration. *How embarrassing.* "A meeting with Aunt Talitha's accountant. But it's nothing I can't handle."

"Are you headed to the shop?"

"I'm about to take my nephew to lunch. This is Will, Jenna's baby."

Daniel stuck his head in the window to look across the headrest into the backseat. "Hey there, Will. I'm Daniel. How old are you?"

Lilly drew away. The man was way too close. And smelled way too good, like shampoo and some expensive cologne. "He's ten months, Daniel. Sorry, but he's not going to hold a conversation with you."

Her comment drew a laugh…and attention from those baby blues. Too close. Entirely too close. And smiling like he cared. Right there in her face, so close he could shift by mere inches and touch his lips to hers and—

She scooted toward the steering wheel, placing

herself at an odd angle, but at least putting distance between them.

Thankfully, he had the sense to know he had invaded her space and hauled himself back out of the window.

She slumped into her seat and nearly gasped out loud as her lungs sucked in air once again. She'd never experienced anyone filling a space quite like Daniel Foreman. Had never had anyone affect her so. And yet, despite his charisma, his regard made her feel...significant. As if he wasn't just trying to charm her, but truly cared.

"Lilly, let me take you and Will to lunch. I'd like to discuss something with you."

Visions of baby food splattering on her face—or, worse, on his—sealed her decision. "Thanks, but no. We wouldn't be good company. Landing food into his mouth can be a challenge."

His eyes sparkled and the faintest of lines crinkled at their edges. "Oh, but, Miss Barnes, I thrive on challenges."

A shiver slid through her—from the cold March air blowing inside, of course. Not the deep timbre of his voice or the fact he seemed to dare her to join him.

She resisted the urge to roll up the window and escape. "I planned to make it quick. I have to get back to the shop to help Jenna."

"I can do quick. I promise not to take much of your time. I'll even help with Will."

Spoken by a man who thought a ten-month-old could tell him his age.

Should she do it?

*You're a businesswoman, Lilly. No longer the shy schoolgirl who hid from handsome guys.* "If you can promise me that we'll be done in less than an hour, we'll join you."

Victory flashed across his face. Or perhaps hope.

"I promise."

"Climb in. I'll drive."

"No need. We're walking over to Frank's. You like pizza?"

He didn't even give her time to answer before he opened Will's door and reached in to get him. He struggled with the buckle a bit, obviously not an expert at child restraint systems. She was about to ask him to move out of the way when the clasp released. Instead of fussing, like she expected Will to do when a total stranger reached for him, he let out a giggle and gave Daniel a slobbery pat on the face.

The little traitor.

"He's cute." Daniel handed Will over and casually wiped his face on the shoulder of his expensive-looking, light tan microfiber jacket, leaving a wet ring. He grabbed the diaper bag. "Need this?"

She took the bag from him and slipped the strap on her shoulder. "Sorry. He's a drooler."

"No problem." He led the way across the street past the courthouse. Frank's red-and-white-striped awning and flashing neon open sign welcomed them.

Once they were seated in a booth in the back corner and had placed Will in a high chair on the end, a man barreled toward them, arms spread wide in welcome. "Daniel, my boy! Who do we have here?"

"Frank, I'd like you to meet Lilly Barnes. Lilly, this is Frank Dellano, the member of my church I told you about."

"Aah, Lilly, nice to meet you!" He warmly gripped both her hands in his and stared into her eyes, his own brown ones encircled by evidence of years of laughter and smiles. "Any friend of Daniel's is a friend of mine. Enjoy your lunch."

"Great place you have here. I'm sure I'll love it."

The waitress, a young, friendly female replica of Frank, took their order, Daniel asking her to put a rush on it if possible. Then he leaned his forearms on the table. "I've been studying your shop."

She dragged away her gaze from his and focused on jars of baby food, opening them. Snapping a bib around Will's neck. "Oh?"

"I noticed you don't have a website. Could really use new, more visible signage. Need to advertise."

Each word out of his mouth shot up her blood pressure another notch. So much to do and with limited funds.

He slid a list toward her. "I can help you increase your business traffic."

The worst part was she suspected she might need help. Though her aunt hadn't been much of a businesswoman, she'd been loving, fun, generous—and talented. Talitha herself had been the business's biggest asset.

A cold fist squeezed inside Lilly's chest. She could never take Talitha's place.

A blob of green beans dripped off Will's chin onto her thumb.

Daniel took hold of her hand and swiped it off with a napkin. Contact with his hand shut out everything else around her. Made her zoom in on the spot where they touched.

That level of awareness disturbed her. She pulled away her hand. "I can clean off my own baby food." When she realized how ridiculous that had sounded, she laughed. "I mean, clean it off myself."

His expression teased, almost as if he understood how he'd affected her. "Just trying to help."

Trying to help feed her nephew. Trying to help run her business. What next? Trying to help run her life?

No, thank you. She'd been there, done that, and had the emotional scars left by an ex-fiancé to prove it.

She might end up having to rent the shop's basement to Daniel. But she didn't need any other involvement with a man who made her heart race just by touching her thumb.

She firmly planted the spoon on the table and steeled herself to look into his gorgeous eyes. "I appreciate your taking the time to evaluate The Yarn

Barn. But I don't think there's anything you can do at this point. We don't have the money."

Daniel opened his mouth to respond, but movement drew his attention away.

"Dada!" Will pursed his lips and blew mashed green bean bubbles that splattered into her face.

Lilly swiped off the mess as the waitress delivered their pizza and her brother-in-law approached his son. The first time they'd seen him since he had left Jenna two days ago.

Daniel let the conversation with Lilly drop and greeted Ned.

Ned ruffled his son's hair and nodded. "Daniel. Lilly."

"Dada!" Will grinned and strained to reach for his father.

"Hang on, big guy." Ned wiped his son's hands and then lifted him out of the high chair. "I'm glad I found you, Lilly. I tried to call earlier, to arrange picking up my boy, here."

Lilly gave her brother-in-law an odd look, as if nervous around him. "I'm sorry. My phone's been off since I met with the accountant."

"Jenna told me that you were in a meeting."

Lilly's eyes lit up. "So you two have talked?"

With red-streaked cheeks, Ned cut a glance at Daniel. "Not really. I called to set up a visit with Will."

A visit? Had he and Jenna separated?

Ned tucked Will under his chin and kissed the top of his head. "I'm sorry I haven't been by. I've been trying to find an apartment."

"Your son misses you. Jenna misses you."

Daniel rose from his seat. "I can take Will and let you two talk."

"No, stay, eat your lunch," Ned said. "You're my pastor. It's time you know what's going on."

Motioning for him to join them, Daniel sat. Lilly scooted over, and Ned, holding his son, slid in the booth beside her. She didn't seem angry with her brother-in-law. If her attitude was any indication of Jenna's, maybe there was hope of reconciliation.

As he and Lilly ate, Ned filled Daniel in.

Ned brushed a finger over his son's arm. "So we've separated. I have to take responsibility for that. But we argued about everything. Then Jenna told me that she didn't need me. That I might as well go ahead and leave."

"Have you had marriage counseling?" Daniel asked.

"She refuses."

Lilly shook out some Cheerios for Will. "She's just scared, you know. Expecting you to leave at any time. She thinks it's easier to push you away before she gets hurt."

Daniel suspected the sisters shared that trait. Maybe from growing up with those "rotten parents"?

"Look, Lilly, I know what a tough childhood you

and Jenna had," Ned said. "But she's pushed me away for a long time. I can't take it anymore." He stood with his son in his arms. "Jenna said it's okay for me to take Will until after dinner."

"He'll enjoy that." Lilly, with a pale face and a sheen of unshed tears in her pretty hazel eyes, gathered Will's diaper bag, then told Ned and Will goodbye.

Daniel said, "I'm sorry your family is struggling right now."

She glanced at him, looked away then once again met his eyes. "We'll make it through."

"A rough childhood makes depending on someone difficult, even when you're all grown up." He touched her hand, couldn't resist offering some sort of comfort.

She glanced down at their hands. "Are you speaking from experience?"

He suddenly recalled his mom sitting in the bleachers alone at football games, an empty seat cushion next to her, the spot his dad had promised to fill. Then after she had died, no one in the bleachers. Frozen dinners alone. His dad coming home and shutting himself in his home office.

He glanced at his watch. "Oh, look. I've almost passed the hour lunch I promised."

She'd turned the tables on him. But he never shared his past with anyone. Daniel had never been able to fill the void after his mother's death, or to pull Blake out of his grief. To share that would be too painful. Especially now. A pastor needed to look capable and inspire confidence if he hoped to help others, to make a difference.

Lilly gave him a look that said she knew he was avoiding the topic.

He simply flagged down the waitress and paid the bill.

As they walked out of Frank's, cold air slapped him in the face. His cell phone vibrated. Normally, he'd ignore it, but the screen showed the caller was Cricket's mother. "Excuse me a second. I need to take this."

On the other end of the line, the woman sobbed uncontrollably. Sick dread slammed him in the gut. "Mrs. Quincy, what's wrong?"

"Cricket took a bunch of pills. We're at the emergency room in Appleton."

"Is she going to be okay?"

"They've given her an antidote that's been pretty successful in similar cases. We have to wait. And pray. Please get Miss Ann to start the prayer chain."

"I will. I'm on my way." *Lord, protect Cricket and the baby. Please let this treatment work.*

Lilly stood beside him, her arms hugged around her waist. "What happened?"

"I need to head to the hospital. A teenage girl from the church is in the ER."

"Do you need a ride?" she asked without any hesitation. A woman who saw a need and jumped in with a solution.

He started to decline, but the offer would save time since he'd walked to town that morning. "Thanks."

They rushed to the car. Lilly backed out of the parking spot, and they sped toward Appleton. He called his grandmother and filled her in, asking her to get the town praying.

"The situation sounds awful. Anything I can do to help?" Lilly asked.

"Nothing. Unless you feel led to pray."

Sick at heart, he stared out the window as they zipped past The Yarn Barn. Surely he could've done more. Could have done something besides set up another meeting for next week. Maybe if he'd called her that morning like he'd meant to…

Except for his brief directions to the hospital, they drove the next ten minutes in silence.

"I hope she'll be okay," Lilly said.

The hospital came into sight. He pointed her toward the emergency entrance. "She's fifteen and pregnant. And I failed her."

"I don't know the whole situation." She reached out and touched his sleeve. "But I know you care. I'm sure that helps. More than you probably realize."

As the car came to a stop out front, their eyes locked, her compassionate gaze soothing him, making him wish for… But at the moment, he had no time for wishing.

He gave her hand a squeeze, a thank-you for understanding him, and then climbed out.

"Wait. Here's my phone number." She jotted it on a piece of scrap paper out of her purse. "Call me when you're ready to leave. Any time, even if it's late."

Touched by her offer, he took the paper. "Thanks for bringing me."

"I'm sure you'll be a comfort to the girl's family."

He shut the door and hurried through the ER entrance. A comfort? How much good was he as a pastor if he hadn't been able to help Cricket see God was big enough to handle her problems, that God had a plan for her life?

Mrs. Quincy paced the floor, a tissue wadded up between her hands, her face streaked with tears. Her pain enough to bring him to his knees, he repeated the prayer circulating in his head. *Lord, don't let Cricket die. Protect her baby.*

He steeled his spine and crossed the waiting room, determined to do more for the hurting teenagers. The kids God had led him to in Corinthia and the neighboring Appleton community had many problems—family struggles, run-ins with the law, failure in school. And Cricket wasn't the only pregnant high schooler.

He couldn't let them down.

The problem was, he was good at starting churches, good at preaching, good at planning outreach ministries. But apparently, when it came to helping the hurting, he fell short.

The pain on Lilly's face whenever she mentioned her childhood etched itself into his brain.

He had to steer clear of beautiful, thoughtful Lilly. Or he would let her down, as well.

## Chapter Three

Lilly couldn't help but worry about Cricket. Yet she was glad she'd been able to take Daniel there, to support her family. He seemed to think he'd failed, but all she saw was a man who cared. Who did what he could to help. Like pray.

The fact Daniel and others, including Ann, were praying for the teen, somehow soothed Lilly.

Thinking of Ann reminded Lilly she needed to ask her to teach knitting classes, so instead of stopping at The Yarn Barn, she bypassed it and headed to town. On the way, she watched for the signage problems Daniel had mentioned.

How had she not noticed that in one direction, they had no store sign at all, and the other, the wooden sign was partially covered? She would have to rectify the situation soon.

When Ann answered her front door, she looked surprised, then pleased. "Lilly, I'm glad you came for the prayer vigil."

Alarm shot through her. "Uh…no. I actually came to ask a huge favor."

"I'll help however I can."

She decided to be direct, honest. "I desperately need your assistance, and Daniel suggested I contact you. I can't knit or crochet, and we need to start holding classes to build community, to keep the business afloat."

Silence. Not good.

"Could you teach? I'll offer you half the class tuition," Lilly said quickly. "And you can pick your hours."

"Oh, it's not the money. I'd be delighted to teach one class a week. But aren't you going to rent out the basement to Daniel? That income would surely help more than one of my classes."

Lilly's heart sank. She'd hoped Ann might teach two or three. "I'm still going through Aunt Talitha's records and am considering renting to the church. If you could teach a class or two, I'd be grateful."

"I think I could manage one every Thursday afternoon. But please take advantage of the rental income." Ann put a firm hand on Lilly's shoulder and gave what she suspected was a stern grandmotherly look. "I'm sure Talitha would want you to honor her agreement with Daniel."

Embarrassment stung Lilly's face. "You're right." Besides, if Ann was only willing to teach one class, they would need that rent money. "Thanks for offering to teach. You're a lifesaver."

The woman's expression morphed into pure happiness. "Good, then. It's settled."

As Lilly drove back to The Yarn Barn, she made plans to locate and organize the tax documents, to try to make sense of all the accountant had told her.

And to inform her sister they would have tenants.

When Lilly walked in the shop, her sister met her at the door.

"The supplier called, the one Aunt Talitha has had for ages. He found out she died, and that you and I placed the recent large order. He's demanding a big payment next week."

Her stomach sank to her toes. "Next week?" The word *week* ended on a squeak. "He always let Talitha pay over ninety days."

Tears filled Jenna's eyes. "I don't know if I can handle one more problem."

Torn, Lilly wasn't sure whether to use tough love or to give Jenna a break. "We're business owners now. We have to handle it."

A spark of irritation flashed in her sister's eyes. *Good.* Irritation was better than the recent sadness.

"It's more than just this place," Jenna said. "My husband left me. *He* left *me.* And he's already insisting on spending time with our child." She let out a quiet sob. "I can't bear thinking of our lives turning into a shared custody agreement."

"You told him to leave." She said it softly, tenderly. "He's apartment hunting. It's time for you ask him to come home."

"Easy for you to say. You've never been married and had to worry about someone you love leaving and breaking your heart."

Lilly's heart squeezed in pain. She'd quit her job and sold her condo to follow her fiancé, Clint, across the country, willing to move even though she'd promised herself she would never move for a man. Only to discover he was uprooting them to hide a fling with a married coworker.

She'd been too humiliated to tell her own sister. Jenna thought Lilly had broken the engagement over the move.

So no, she had never married. But she knew about the loss of hopes and dreams, knew the pain of betrayal and a broken heart.

Lilly pushed away the painful memories. "I may not know exactly what you're going through, but I know your son needs you. And I need you. So you can't let this knock you down. I raised you to be stronger than this."

Jenna mumbled something about Lilly not being her mother as she busied herself straightening the yarn bins.

"Now, little sister, I suggest you go after your husband and work out your problems. Before he leases that apartment. Because, I tell you what. The man looked miserable today. He misses you."

Jenna glanced up, stricken. "Does he really? You're not just saying that?"

"He really does."

Jenna pulled her cell phone out of her pocket. "I doubt he'll answer if I call."

"You won't know until you try."

"You're right. Maybe I'll talk to him when he brings Will home."

"Good for you. Now...I came in here to tell you Ann is only willing to teach one class a week. So I think we should honor Aunt Talitha's promise to rent the basement to the church."

Jenna's green eyes looked huge in her pale face. "Lilly, are we going to make it? The shop, I mean. Because I can't bear to think we might lose it."

They wouldn't lose it if Lilly could help it. Determined to use her good business sense, and not the emotions that seemed to have taken over since Daniel first walked through the door, she made a vow to put the shop first. "We'll be fine if we rent to Daniel's church. He's even offered to have his church members begin refinishing the basement, taking expenses for supplies out of the rent money. Using volunteer labor."

"Sounds like it's a deal we can't refuse."

"I agree. And if we ask for a security deposit, maybe we'll have enough to pay the supplier, or at least get him off our back." As much as she'd like to resist having him around, and resist changing her plan for the basement, she needed to make wise choices.

As Lilly dug through boxes of Talitha's records for the next few hours, she considered her options for marketing the store. Daniel had been right. She needed to make the shop more visible. Needed to consider inexpensive and free advertising. With his office in her basement, she'd have easy access to his advice…should she choose to take it.

*Daniel.* She couldn't shake him from her mind.

The man sat at the hospital in an impossible situation with that poor family. They probably hadn't had dinner. And he would need a ride home.

*This is not good.* She had to quit thinking about him. The man was too attractive for his own good. For *her* own good.

And he was kind and good and, she suspected, trustworthy. All dangerous, because those qualities made her want to know him better. To spend time with him.

She should call and offer to take by some sandwiches. See if he—they—needed anything. To try to be a friend to him—them.

Or course, anything beyond friendship wasn't wise. Because once she and Jenna revived the business and sold it into capable hands, she would be taking her half of the proceeds and returning to Kentucky to follow her own dream. Of starting work as a freelance photojournalist.

Once the terms of Talitha's will were fulfilled, she intended to leave Corinthia—with her heart intact.

\* \* \*

Nothing in seminary had prepared Daniel for sitting in an ICU waiting room with parents whose daughter—and unborn grandchild—might die.

But, praise God, they'd survived.

"So they think Cricket will fully recover?" Lilly asked as she drove him back to GranAnn's house, her presence easing his earlier despair.

"The antidote they administered was successful. The main worry now is the possibility of long-term effects of the acetaminophen overdose on the baby. Won't know anything until after he's born."

"Scary stuff." She glanced his way, light from streetlamps flickering on her face. "It's a boy?"

"Yeah. We'll keep praying."

Her gaze darted away like it did anytime he mentioned prayer. He wished she would talk to him about what had happened that turned her away from her faith.

As they neared his grandmother's house, he spotted his dad's car. Daniel dreaded what would undoubtedly end up as a confrontation.

Lilly parked but left the car running. He hopped out and walked around to the driver's side. Opened her door and held out his hand, hoping she'd join him under the beautiful blanket of stars.

She hesitated but ultimately turned off the car and stepped out.

"Thanks again for offering to bring dinner tonight. The Quincys were grateful."

"No biggie." She glanced away as if embarrassed.

"Seems you're good at being thoughtful, taking care of others."

With a shrug, she proved she had trouble accepting praise.

"I've just always stepped in when needed." Her quiet laugh hinted at hurt.

"No, it's more than that. I suspect it was in your nature all along."

Cold, brisk wind whipped her hair into her face. She cinched it with her hand into a ponytail and held on. She looked into his eyes, and he felt the same connection he'd felt when he'd first met her, as if something simmered below the surface. Something neither of them was willing to examine.

"Thanks for bringing me home," he said.

"No problem."

"Come on, Lilly. Try accepting my thanks and saying, 'You're welcome, Daniel.'" As he grinned at her, a piece of her hair escaped her grasp. He brushed it behind her ear.

A thrill jolted through him at the contact. Then fear followed the same route.

She laughed but stepped out of touching range. She bowed with a flourish. "You're welcome, Daniel. And now I have something that'll make your day even better."

He stuffed his hands into the pockets of his jacket, a reminder not to touch. "What's that?"

"After a little...uh, prompting from Ann, Jenna and I talked this afternoon. We need the income from rent, and you made a tempting offer to renovate the place."

He shook his head, incredulous. Leave it to Gran to fix a situation he couldn't fix. Then again, she probably had ulterior motives. "You're accepting the offer?"

"Yep. We'd like you to move in and renovate the space."

"It's a deal." He reached out quickly to shake on it before she changed her mind.

With a laugh, she hesitated, staring at his outstretched hand. When she tentatively took his hand, his heart thumped in his chest, as if the moment were momentous, more than a business deal. Silly, of course, but no less jarring.

The temptation to pull her into his arms nearly overwhelmed his good sense. He ground his teeth and jammed his hand in his pocket. "We'll be good tenants. And I'll do a good job with the work, keeping costs low."

"We can talk details and contracts later, after this crisis with Cricket is over."

"I think we're past the immediate crisis." He shook his head and glanced skyward, praying once again for her and the baby. "But she has a long way to go."

"You didn't let her down, you know. She needed medical help, not a pastor."

Spoken by a woman who didn't think she needed God. "I appreciate your take on the situation. But I feel like I need to do more, though I'm just not sure how."

"You'll figure it out. You have a good heart, and Cricket is lucky to have you on her side." She slid into the driver's seat.

He leaned inside. "Thanks again for the ride. Your support today meant a lot to me."

"No pr—" She gave a sweet laugh. "I was glad to help."

Her laugh wrapped around his heart like a balm. Which terrified him. He couldn't afford to be attracted to someone, especially someone who didn't believe as he did, didn't have faith in God. When the stray hair blew in her face once again, he forced himself to ignore it.

He put his hand on the door, preparing to close it. "You won't regret allowing the church to meet in your basement. We'll move on when we find a permanent location. And actually, I'll move on before that."

"What do you mean?"

"My calling is to start churches. Once this one is running smoothly, I'll move on and start another."

As if he'd pushed a button, her expression chilled. Gone was the teasing laughter, the warm camaraderie.

"I see," she said. "So you're here temporarily, as well."

"Yes. In fact, I've already had a congregation in South Georgia ask me to move down there to start an inner-city mission church."

"How soon will you go?"

For the second time, he had a flicker of doubt. Wondered if he could've misread his calling. "Hard to say. We have a couple more projects to get off the ground here."

She clutched the door handle. "Well, good luck to you."

"I'll be in touch about a rental contract."

"Come by on Monday if you'd like." The invitation was in her most businesslike voice.

At least Daniel had secured the church's location for the near future. He didn't plan to tell the congregation about it until he had the contract in writing, though. Too many variables, including the fact that Lilly could back out at any moment.

Yes, they had a business relationship. Short-term. Then why the attraction? Why the worry over her reaction to the fact he would eventually head south? Moving on was what he did, what he was good at.

Lilly Barnes was a distraction he couldn't afford.

Lights and the sound of the television in the family room drew Daniel. GranAnn sat in her chair watching her favorite news channel. His dad read the paper.

"I'm home." Daniel kissed his grandmother's cheek. "Cricket's going to be okay."

Ann clasped her hands together at her chest. "Oh, thank You, Lord."

"Hello, Dad."

"Daniel." He nodded a greeting. No hug. No hand-shake. "So what happened with the girl? I thought you said you'd been counseling her. Now I hear she tried to kill herself?"

Daniel clenched his jaw, chomping down on the words that nearly flew out of his mouth. "I'm surprised to see you here this late. Were you waiting to see me?" He despised how pathetically hopeful he sounded, as if he hadn't had the same smack down over and over.

Gran reached for Daniel's hand. "Yes, son, he was. I'll let you two talk." She patted his cheek and then left the room.

Daniel sat in Gran's worn green recliner and faced his father.

Methodically, as if taking a moment to gather his thoughts, Blake folded the newspaper, pressing the creases to hold them in place. A man who worried about insignificant details, forgetting what was important.

"I came to let you know I've found you a building to rent. It's a vacant gas station over in Appleton."

Daniel sucked in a breath and held it. He should say something. But he couldn't.

"Don't look so shocked. I do have connections around here, you know."

"It's not that. It's..." For the first time in ages, he wanted to smile at his father. "Thank you. I appreciate the help. More than you know. But I've gotten the okay to rent from Lilly and her sister at The Yarn Barn."

"Have you signed a contract yet?"

"No, sir. But we have a verbal agreement. I plan to honor that." Especially since Gran seemed to think Lilly and Jenna needed the income.

Blake's face turned red. His cheeks puffed out with air, as if trying to hold back angry words.

"I'm sorry, Dad. But thanks for your effort."

He slapped the newspaper on the end table. "I hope you don't regret it. That yarn place is a dump. Looks like it's falling down."

"It's actually structurally sound. And the outside has recently been painted."

"I bet she'll overcharge you. You don't even know this girl." Blake stood regally, but indignation rolled off him in waves. He stalked away, and a moment later, the front door slammed.

Daniel rushed outside and caught up to him before he could close his car door. Blake had made an effort. Daniel needed to try to, as well. "Dad, I'm sorry. Please stay. I'd like to tell you more about my plans for the church."

Blake stared out the car windshield. Didn't acknowledge his son. He paused for about three seconds as if making a decision, and then he closed the door.

Daniel stood on the pavement, the cold wind cutting through his shirt, as the car backed down the driveway. His dad had always been such a strong man. With broad shoulders and a confident gait, he had a powerful air about him. Blake felt in control of his world, and some called him arrogant.

But tonight, he'd taken the time to wait around for Daniel. Had made a move to help him. Could he be trying to reconcile? Yet, earlier, his dad hinted at Daniel's failure in counseling Cricket.

Daniel sighed, his breath fogging in front of his face. He tried not to expect much from his dad. But he craved the man's respect, hoped that someday he'd earn it.

To earn respect, Blake's or anyone else's for that matter, Daniel had to do better at his job. Needed to better serve the people in the community. If he could just find some way to minister to the increasing number of hurting people he'd come in contact with.

Maybe if Cricket hadn't felt so alone… Maybe if she'd had a support group she wouldn't be lying in a hospital bed in the ICU.

An idea began to take shape as his dad's taillights disappeared from sight. But the plan would require a favor from Lilly Barnes.

And he suspected that with this, even Lilly, who always rushed to help, would think he was asking too much.

Lilly felt as conspicuous as a slice of pepperoni on a veggie pizza. She practically dragged Jenna and Will toward a table in the far corner of Daniel's "church" to the only empty seats she spotted. Frank's Pizza Place was packed for the Sunday morning worship service, so they hadn't stood a chance of slipping in unnoticed.

A woman they squeezed by said, "Welcome," and gave Lilly's arm a friendly pat. Others smiled, obviously curious. Embarrassed to be the object of attention, she tugged harder to hurry Jenna toward the two chairs.

"You don't have to pull off my arm," Jenna whispered, her eyes flashing. "I'm as nervous about this as you are."

Not nervous enough to keep her from waking Lilly at the crack of dawn, using old-fashioned guilt to try to coerce her into coming. *Will needs to have the roots we never had,* she'd said.

That was at least partially true. Will did need roots, something she and Jenna had desperately craved as their dad had moved them from one city to another, blaming others for his job failures, looking for some pie in the sky that never materialized.

But Lilly didn't think taking the boy to church would fill that need. When she'd refused, Jenna begged her to come with them to the worship service to see Ned. To prove to him that Jenna was trying to change.

The real reason for Jenna's sudden urge for church attendance.

Honestly, did Jenna think showing up once for a service would send her husband rushing home, begging her to take him back?

Still, Lilly hadn't been able to refuse. She wanted to collapse as they reached their chairs and pulled off their coats, but the people were standing, singing.

"Where's Ned?" Jenna mouthed.

Lilly scanned the crowd but didn't see him. Had they come for nothing?

After two songs that Lilly and Jenna didn't know, Daniel came to the front of the room—no pulpit in this church—and spoke without the aid of a microphone. He welcomed everyone, and she knew the exact moment he spotted her. His eyes widened and one side of his mouth hitched up in that crooked smile that always arrowed straight to her belly.

She tried to deflect that arrow, reminding herself what he'd told her two nights before. Daniel was a church starter. He would soon move on. And then move again. And again. He was not the kind of man whose smile should make her stomach flutter.

His expression softened when he noticed Jenna and Will. Will, who had refused to stay with the nursery worker over in the side dining room. Will, who would most likely cause a fuss before the end of the service.

Why on earth had she let Jenna guilt her into coming?

*Roots.* For Will…for Jenna. And maybe hope for a flailing marriage.

Lilly would tolerate anything to make sure Jenna was settled and happy before it was time to sell the shop and move on to pursue her own dreams.

Daniel's deep voice drew in Lilly despite her desire to send her mind wandering off elsewhere. His message—and the type of love he spoke about, God's love—sucked her right in. As if she were an arid desert and his words rain.

She tried to ignore the yearning that suddenly made it hard to breathe. She bit her lip, and dug the fingernails of her right hand into her left palm, fighting tears.

*No.* She slammed a wall around her heart. Refused to listen. She wanted to hold her hands over her ears and shout *la la la la* to block out Daniel's words. Instead, she thought of the chorus of her favorite country music song and, in her mind, sang it as loudly as she could. Thankfully, Daniel appeared to be winding down.

She looked at Jenna, who had a tear trailing down her cheek. Oh, no. Lilly had to get a grip on her own emotions for Jenna's sake.

Will wiggled and whimpered. *Yes.* The perfect distraction. She took him from Jenna and held him in her lap. He stood and bounced, his face turning red and scrunching up as if working up to a good cry. Everything else faded into the background. Finally.

Will let out a wail. "Eeeee," he whined.

Laughter sounded around the room and Jenna frantically dug in the diaper bag for the container of Cheerios.

"I'm hungry, too, Will." Daniel rubbed his hand over his jaw stifling a laugh. "Time to tie this up, anyway." He raised his arms. "Stand with me, and let's pray."

When everyone stood, Jenna grabbed Lilly's arm. Tears poured down her sister's cheeks, her shoulders lifting in jerky shudders as if she was desperately trying to hold herself together. "I'm leaving." She slipped away and rushed out the door.

Was Jenna crying over Ned? Or had she had a spiritual breakthrough? The latter scared Lilly silly. How could she possibly understand and help?

The words Daniel had spoken nudged once again at Lilly's heart, reminding her that if Will hadn't called out, she might be in the same condition as her sister.

Rather than risk staying through the prayer, Lilly grabbed their stuff and hurried out. She opened the car and found Jenna sobbing.

Jenna shielded her face. "Don't let Will see me, it'll upset him."

Lilly shut the door and stood outside the pizza

parlor, Will on her hip, trying to decide what to do. She peeked in the restaurant window and watched as the church people hugged and laughed and talked. A variety of people from all walks of life. Also several young families. A group Ned and Jenna could fit in with.

After a few minutes, her sister's crying hadn't stopped. Lilly decided maybe she should go inside and find Daniel. She was out of her league and probably needed backup. As she entered and slinked toward the kitchen, Frank spotted her.

"Aah, Lilly! So glad you joined us today. Are you staying for pizza?"

"Um, no. Is there somewhere I can wait for Daniel?"

Frank tossed a pizza crust in the air. "Go on over. Talk to him."

"No, I don't want to interrupt."

His sympathetic expression told her that he understood.

"Daniel may be a while. They visit till I run them off when customers arrive." Frank nodded at Will. "But you take the boy and wait in his office." He nodded toward the back of the restaurant, then turned to the brick oven where he pushed in a paddle and came out with a luscious-looking pizza. The smell of oozing cheese made her mouth water.

As she headed down the narrow hallway, Frank greeted incoming customers. "Aah, Mark and Hannah! Kids! I have your regular table waiting for you!"

Had Lilly ever had a regular table anywhere? What would that be like to be known…expected? She brushed off the crazy longing to have a place like that.

She and Will passed the restrooms and a storage closet.

An open door caught her eye. She peeked into a cramped, little corner room and found what must be Daniel's desk. She entered and sat across from it, dug out the container of Cheerios and fed them to Will to pacify him until they could have lunch.

Daniel's desk was stacked with several notepads with pages flipped back to hold his place. Pens and pencils lay scattered. Sticky notes were plastered all over a whiteboard, arrows and words jotted around them.

Her stomach plummeted. How many times had she seen her father's desk in much the same condition? Her dad circling the threadbare rug at home with a notepad in hand, mumbling one scheme after another for taking small town, USA, by storm.

Any connection she'd felt with Daniel slipped away like a dropped stitch, leaving disappointment lodged in her chest. She could almost see the gears turning in his head. The man was a dreamer. Shouldn't she have expected this after hearing he liked to start new projects?

She could imagine his quest.

Another soul won. Another small business saved.

Another needy person helped—like Cricket…or Lilly.

Disgust churned in her gut. She didn't want to ask him to help Jenna. Sharing the basement of her building with him would be taxing enough.

She stood, ready to escape and deal with Jenna by herself, and nearly ran into Daniel.

He turned to avoid a collision as he squeezed by her. "Oh, hi, Lilly. You're just the person I wanted to see." He pointed her to the chair she'd vacated and then leaned on his desk, crossing his legs. "I'm glad you came today."

His eyes were warm, welcoming, as if he meant what he'd said. She nearly let it suck her in. She reminded herself why she was there. "Jenna hoped to see Ned." And the venture had been wasted.

"I'm sorry. Ned got called in to work." Daniel reached behind him and grabbed one of his notepads, flipped two pages over. When he looked up, his blue eyes shone like when she'd first met him.

Maybe she should renege on the offer to rent to him. She needed stable. Calm. Reliable. Not this new version of Daniel so like her dad.

Awkward silence hung between them as he stared into her eyes.

Unable to stand another instant, she said, "So… what's on your paper?"

"Cricket's situation inspired me to brainstorm ways to help her and other girls."

*Uh-oh.* She stood up and tucked Will against her

hip. "Look, I don't know where this is leading, but I need to go. Jenna's waiting in the car, and Will needs his nap."

He'd used two of the five words that had always instilled dread in Lilly: *inspire* and *brainstorm*. The other three were *dream, opportunity* and—

He reached out to stop her, setting his hand lightly on her arm. "Please hear me out. I have an idea for a project. And I need your help."

—and *idea*.

He'd used three of her dad's favorite buzzwords. Words that always ended up making Lilly's life miserable.

And she'd offered to let him share her building?

She wouldn't be a part of his plan, no matter how good it sounded. She had more on her plate than she could handle. And a sister in the car sobbing, to boot.

"No, Daniel. I'm sorry, but I really have to go."

On Monday, she was supposed to sign a contract with Reverend Daniel Foreman. What on earth had she gotten herself into?

# Chapter Four

Daniel stood across from Lilly at The Yarn Barn sales counter with pen in hand, ready to sign the contract before she could change her mind.

She slid one copy of the stapled papers across to him. "It's very basic. I found the template online. Let me know if you see anything I've forgotten."

He gave it a thorough reading. "Looks like you covered the bases." And, surprisingly, hadn't put a time limit on the rental. "I plan to have our church treasurer sign as well since I don't know how long I'll be here. We can add another line for him."

"That's fine."

"I wanted him on the contract, too. For continuity."

Frosty hazel eyes speared him. "Yes, continuity... people who can manage to stay in one place for a while."

Her disapproving tone reminded him of his dad, sending ripples of frustration through him. He wanted to tell her that she had no right to judge him or his calling. But instead, he calmly said, "Care to explain why you have such a problem with me leaving once the church is well established?"

Her face reddened, and she crossed her arms so tightly he wondered how she could breathe. The issue was obviously personal to her.

"Never mind," he said. "Doesn't matter how you feel about me personally." He quickly signed and dated both copies, and then slid the papers back to her.

When she didn't move, he offered his pen. Had his temper messed up everything?

She took a deep breath. "I'm sorry if I sound judgmental. I can't help disliking when people leave every time opportunity strikes."

"Did I hit a nerve—someone in your life?"

She straightened two pens lying on the counter, chewed her lip. "My dad."

So he was right about the personal part. "You've hinted at a difficult childhood. Did your father leave you?"

Pain sparked in her eyes, then faded to flatness. "No, not physically."

When she didn't elaborate, he waited, staring at her profile as she gazed across the shop.

She huffed out a frustrated breath. "He was a dreamer, okay?" She glared at him as if angry at him for pushing her. "A dreamer who blamed others for his failures and uprooted us over and over, looking for the next sure thing."

Having her categorize him with her father, who'd made life miserable for his family, disturbed him. Deeply.

He leaned on the counter so he could look into her eyes. "Lilly, I'm not being lured away by the church in South Georgia. I won't leave until we've accomplished our goals here."

"I'm assuming your church knows your plan?"

"Yes. I've been up front from day one. Told them my vision for my ministry."

She uncrossed her arms, but she still didn't accept his pen. "Do you think they really understand? That they truly comprehend you mean to leave as quickly as you can? Because I can't imagine throwing myself into something, behind *someone,* when I knew at any moment he'd walk away."

What could he say to that? She had her opinions, and he wouldn't be swaying them anytime soon. He once again offered his pen.

Her mouth tilted in a semblance of a smile as she took his pen, but he had the distinct impression she didn't relish the idea of binding herself to him.

Or, rather, to his church.

He had to remember that. She wasn't signing an agreement with him personally.

She scrawled her signature. Once on the church's copy. Once on hers.

"I'll ask the treasurer to drop by sometime today

if possible." Time to get down to business. To ignore the disappointment eating at him. Why should he care how his landlord felt about him?

He pulled a measuring tape from his pocket and pointed to the basement door. "Do you mind?"

"Go ahead. There's a door around back that leads directly to the basement. I'll get another copy of the key made so you can come and go as you please."

She obviously didn't want him in her way. He'd be happy to oblige. "Thanks."

As he started down the stairs, a wall of cool, damp air smacked into him.

"So when do you think you'll move in?" Lilly called.

"I plan to bring the three high school boys I mentor to help after school this week. Other church members are ready to jump in, as well. My goal is to hold our first service here this Sunday."

She gave a barely detectable sigh. "Wow, that quickly. I look forward to seeing the revamped space."

"It won't be totally done by Sunday. But if all goes well, it'll be good enough for us to meet here."

She clamped her lips together, but a hint of dimple dipped in her cheek. "So I guess Frank will be relieved to have his restaurant back. And you won't have to smell pizza cooking."

"Yeah. No more stomachs growling during the sermon."

When she released her hold on the smile, it

slammed into him. Was she trying, in her teasing, to make up for accusing him of being like her father?

He headed down the steps, trying to ignore the fact he cared so much about her opinion of him.

Lilly paced the uneven wood floor of The Yarn Barn, her stomach as nervous as the first day of school in a new town. When a hammer pounded downstairs, she flinched.

"Do you think anyone will show?" Jenna gnawed on her thumbnail.

Lilly took Jenna's hand and pulled it away from her mouth, giving a gentle, reassuring squeeze. Faking a confident smile as she smoothed the wrinkles out of her gray wool trousers. "We did all we could to promote our class on short notice. I put up flyers everywhere. Even at the mega craft store in Appleton."

Jenna giggled. "Don't imagine those lasted long."

Despite the nerves, Lilly was hopeful. "For some reason, I feel good about this. As if everything is about to turn around for us."

"I hope you're right. I need some good news."

The pounding in the basement made Lilly cringe. "No progress with Ned?"

Jenna shook her head as she scooted folding chairs around a plastic rectangular table she'd set up earlier. "He talks to me all stiff and formal, as if we barely know each other. And he only calls when he wants to talk about Will."

"At least you're on speaking terms." She hit the start button on the coffeepot. As it hissed and gurgled, Ann arrived.

Lilly hurried over to greet her. "Thanks so much for coming."

"It's nice to be back here," Ann said with tears in her eyes. "I'm pleased you girls decided to take over the shop. Talitha would be proud."

Lilly reached out to take Ann's box of supplies and carry it for her. "I guess that'll depend on how successful we are in turning around the business."

"Hi, Miss Ann," Jenna called from the corner gathering area. "We're meeting over here."

"I heard about their separation," Ann whispered. "I'm praying God will show them the way."

Lilly didn't know how to respond, so she nodded and then hauled the box to the corner of the shop. As she set it down, a loud bang sounded downstairs. Then the incessant pounding began once again.

"Oh, it sounds like my grandson is at work." Ann's eyes sparkled as if ecstatic that Daniel had been banging away all day with a hammer, startling everyone.

Lilly had hoped he'd be done before class started.

The front door opened again and Lilly greeted the customer.

"I'm here for the class," said the woman, probably in her late fifties, with perfectly styled, highlighted blond hair, wearing what looked like a hand-knit jacket. Very nicely done—obviously not a beginner.

"I've been looking for a new group and saw your ad." She smiled and pulled a canvas bag higher on her shoulder.

"I'm Lilly Barnes, one of the new owners." She shook the woman's hand.

"Nice to meet you. I'm Vera."

Lilly introduced Vera to Jenna and Ann, and then offered her a cup of coffee as they gathered around the table.

When Vera pulled out a huge project—a gorgeous gray shawl in a complicated pattern on a circular needle, Lilly's face burned. She, part owner of the shop, would have to reveal her measly beginner scarf. And the other owner would have to admit she didn't knit or crochet at all. They weren't exactly representing their business well.

"That's beautiful," Lilly said.

"Thanks. I'd set it aside for a while to work on a blanket for a friend's baby. But I'm finally back at it. I love working with a group." She glanced around the room, no doubt looking for the rest of the *group*.

"We're glad you're here. This is the first class since my sister and I took over the shop. I'm not sure if anyone else is coming today." Or ever.

"I doubt I can teach you anything," Ann said as she pulled out her own project, a baby hat in the softest of pale pink yarns. "But it'll be fun to watch you work."

Vera's hands began to move in smooth, quick motions. She barely looked at the needles as she flew through the stitches. "I don't really need the class. I'm just thankful for the opportunity for company."

Which, Lilly recognized, validated her desire to eventually open the basement for building a knitting community.

Daniel gave a couple good whacks of his hammer to confirm her realization.

"No need to pay tuition for the class," Lilly said, her heart sinking. She slid a sign-up form across the table. "You can fill out this registration card before you leave so we can contact you for special events. Feel free to hang out here anytime you like."

"Oh, no. I want to officially sign up. If all goes well, I plan to invite some friends. It'll be fun to have weekly classes together."

If all goes well? Meaning she'd invite only if she liked the place? Two sharp raps on the wall made Lilly jump.

Vera flinched as she wrote down her information. "Although, not if it's noisy and hard on my nerves. The last yarn shop we frequented added a coffee shop. The patrons got too loud."

Lilly glanced at her ancient coffeepot and figured they wouldn't be drawing a noisy crowd.

The front door opened again, ringing the little bell she'd placed on it. A split second later, Will woke from his nap behind the counter and wailed.

From the look on Vera's face, her nerves were mightily jangled.

Like Lilly's.

"Helloooo," called an elderly woman from the front of the store.

After reassuring Vera that Will would settle down soon, and that the construction was temporary, she excused herself to attend to the customer, who'd come for the class.

"I've always wanted to knit," the woman named Flo said in a loud, boisterous voice, her shining blue eyes and grin making for a jovial expression. "I've taken a couple classes but never quite caught on. Maybe you'll be the one who'll finally get it through my thick skull." She gave a hearty laugh, and Lilly couldn't help but like her.

They would have a lot of fun with Flo. If she didn't get on Vera's tender nerves.

Once Flo registered and paid, she picked out a skein of yarn and pair of needles. They gathered around the table, and Ann began teaching Flo how to cast on.

The next hour flew by, punctuated by banging from downstairs and Flo's guffaws whenever she dropped a stitch. Vera pled a headache and left a bit early. Lilly wouldn't be surprised if she never came back.

When the class was over, Flo gathered her new supplies. "I enjoyed it, ladies. I look forward to next week."

They had two class members, one with her own supplies and no need to buy more anytime soon. Disappointment churned in Lilly's belly. Looked as if her dream of growing business through a thriving community might not materialize anytime soon... if ever.

A good thing they'd decided to rent the basement.

"Well, I know you're probably disappointed in the turnout," Ann said as she gathered her things and put them back in the box. "But I think that went well. It'll probably grow, especially as they tell their friends."

"Do you think so? Vera wasn't too pleased about the noise."

Ann waved away the worry. "I can tell she'll always find something to gripe about. Don't fret about her."

Still, the lukewarm response to the class worried Lilly.

"So how have you and Daniel been getting along?" Ann asked, that same twinkle in her eyes as if she knew some kind of insider information on her grandson.

"I haven't seen him much since Monday. He's been using the back door, working day in and day out."

Ann patted Lilly's cheek. "You two should grab some dinner tonight. Tell him I won't be cooking. I have a meeting to attend."

"Okay." She would tell him about Ann's meeting. But she wouldn't be having dinner with him.

By the time Ann left and Jenna had headed home

with Will, Lilly was dying to see the results of all that pounding around the basement walls and ceiling.

A whack of the hammer thumped right below Lilly's feet, making her jump. She headed down the stairs to the basement. "Your grandmother said to tell you she's not cooking tonight. And that's about all that racket I can take," she hollered. She laughed as she rounded the corner to where Daniel stood on a ladder.

His face lit up like his grandmother's. "Oh, hi, Lilly. How'd the new class go?"

"Not well."

He climbed down the ladder and set aside his hammer. "I'm sorry. What happened?" His stance was wide and strong. When he crossed his arms, it highlighted his bulging biceps, making her heart skitter and her breathing grow shallow.

"Only two showed…and, uh…" She focused her eyes upward onto his face. His concern touched her, made her long to have someone to share burdens with, to lean on.

Reality check. This man was a pastor. He had that concerned expression down to an art. "And one of the attendees startled every time you banged your hammer. Which was about six thousand times."

He tried to bite his lip, but his gorgeous, crooked smile won out. Then he laughed.

His laughter was as appealing as his big strong shoulders. Both proved powerful and drew her toward him. "Don't laugh." She glanced up at him, then let her eyes flutter downward, realizing even as she did it, that she was flirting, couldn't help herself.

"Since one of the women has *delicate nerves,*" she added, "you may have messed up my chances for a successful class, you know."

"You don't say." He leaned in. She wasn't the only one flirting.

The connection they'd shared since day one swirled in the air around them. She imagined two vines reaching toward each other, mingling, twining around each other.

He blinked. Took a deep breath. Stepped away. "I'm truly sorry for the commotion. But look around." He pointed all along the ceiling. "We're nearly finished with the drop ceiling grid."

*We?* She glanced around. And sure enough, there were two teenage boys across the room who'd stopped to stare. Then Frank stuck his head out of a little room they'd built and winked.

Her face burned hot as a fireplace poker. She gave an awkward wave. "Sorry. Y'all carry on."

She hurried back up the steps, mortification making her want to cry.

Daniel caught up to her as she slipped behind the counter. "I'm sorry. I should have told you they were there. I was just…well…um, distracted."

Tears burned her nose. She hated to make a spectacle. More than anything, though, she didn't want to feel so drawn to a man who was completely wrong for her. Or to any man for that matter. "Tell them I didn't mean to sound unappreciative. I was joking about the noise."

"The kids won't care. And Frank…well, he'll rib me about us. But you're safe." Red streaked across his cheeks.

Daniel's reassurance made her heart dance around in her chest. He was such a nice guy, trying to make her feel better after she'd pretty much thrown herself at him.

He leaned his forearms on the countertop, his expression turned serious. "So you didn't have a good turnout?"

She let out a huge sigh that had been weighing on her throughout the class. "No. Only the two, and one of them is practically a pro."

"So it didn't generate much income."

"Unfortunately, no. I'm going to have to figure out a way to increase enrollment."

He raised an eyebrow. "I offered to help."

"Oh, that's right. You have a marketing background. In what?"

"Sports management."

How on earth could that help? She lifted both hands palm up as if they were a scale. She raised one higher. "Sports management." Then she raised the other. "Yarn shop."

His lip quirked up at one corner. "I promise I can help."

But at what cost? She truly doubted his help would be worth the risk to her heart if she spent any more time with him than necessary. The only thing she considered necessary was incidental contact as they went about their daily business.

She wouldn't expose herself on purpose to a charming dreamer any more than she'd expose herself to a contagious disease.

"Score it across the line like this," Daniel said to the two high school guys who'd come again after school to help. On a Friday, no less. He raked his blade across the ceiling tile.

The boys, from broken, troubled homes, had impressed him already with their commitment to the mentoring sessions week after week, even though Ian had stated the desire to quit. And now they'd shown up an extra day to help with the renovation.

"Then I snap it apart?" asked towheaded Parker Pruitt, the younger of the two at fifteen and a half. Parker had proved himself to be independent from his troublemaking older brothers and would most likely overcome his family legacy.

"Yep. Give it a try."

Doubt filled his gray-blue eyes. "What if I mess it up?"

"Come on, man," Ian Thomas said, grabbing it out of Parker's hand. "We'll be here all night if you worry about every little piece."

Ian, with his dark eyes, dark hair and matching dark attitude, was seventeen and had anger issues. Ian wanted to drop out of school, and likely drop off

the map. Daniel had worked hard to keep him mo-
tivated to earn his diploma and was surprised the
young man was still hanging around.

With a sure snap, Ian broke the tile and started
on the next. Undeterred by the censure, Parker followed suit and soon built his own pile of tile blocks
sized to install along the ceiling edges.

Daniel still planned to be finished in time to have
services here on Sunday. But his to-do list was long,
including purchasing and setting up tables, chairs,
dehumidifiers and space heaters. Plus, if they had
time, he wanted to paint the drywall.

He'd begun to doubt they'd finish by Sunday. Especially since his third worker, seventeen-year-old
Ricky Hartley, who'd been sentenced to community
service for excessive speeding, hadn't shown up.

Daniel had agreed to supervise the kid as a favor
to his grandmother's pastor, Phil Hartley, who
served the church in downtown Corinthia. The boy
was Phil's nephew, and the pastor and his wife had
petitioned for legal guardianship.

"Can we start putting in the tiles?" Parker asked.

"Sure, in the center of the room. We'll do the
outer tiles after painting."

Parker grabbed a ladder and hurried up the rungs,
the ladder tilting to one side.

"Whoa! Slow down or we'll end up at the ER fixing that hard head of yours."

The boy snickered but slowed his ascension up

the ladder. "My mom says there ain't nothin' harder than a Pruitt boy's head."

"With four Pruitt men under her roof, she's certainly the expert."

As Parker and Ian worked, Daniel's disappointment in Ricky grew. He still hadn't shown, and now Daniel would have to report him to the caseworker.

He strode to his newly framed and Sheetrock-enclosed office to finish adjustments on the newly installed door. He'd have to call Phil, too. The poor man wanted better for his nephew. But the boy was nearly eighteen. It might be too late to help him.

"This one fit!" Parker gave a fist pump and wobbled on the ladder.

"Great," Ian mumbled. "He's going to celebrate each stupid tile."

Daniel laughed. He was proud of how far the teens had come, especially Ian, who would have cursed at the younger boy just weeks ago. "Patience, my man. I seem to remember a similar situation involving a passing grade on a cooking assignment in Family and Consumer Science class."

Ian bit back a smile. "That's different. Cooking's stupid."

"Let me see…" He looked at the ceiling as if thinking. "I seem to remember something similar you said about the tiles…."

The boy chuckled, his brown eyes flashing with humor. "You got me." He climbed the ladder, placed a tile, then did a silent celebration imitating Parker.

Parker good-naturedly fist bumped him. "Nice work, dude."

"Daniel," Lilly called from upstairs.

Footsteps followed. They weren't Lilly's. Heavy boots clunked down toward them.

When he turned, he found Lilly standing in front of Ricky. She didn't look happy.

"What happened?" Daniel asked.

"Can we talk in your office?"

He showed her and Ricky to the small room and shut the door.

"Mr. Attitude here got mouthy with my customers," she said.

"I didn't do nothin'," Ricky said, towering over Lilly, who barely reached his shoulder.

"Then what do you call the insults you launched?" Lilly asked.

"I came in looking for Daniel. Not that it's any of your business."

Daniel shook his head at the boy's rudeness. "Ricky, that's enough. It *is* Ms. Barnes's business. She owns this place."

Ricky shrugged as if he couldn't care less. "Whatever."

"You're late," Daniel said. "In fact, I don't know if we can count today toward your community service."

"Come on, man. I tried to find it. But when I walked in and saw a bunch of blue-haired women, I thought I was at the wrong place."

Daniel widened his eyes at Lilly, questioning.

He thought he spotted a glimmer of humor behind the stern look. "A couple of your church ladies dropped by to check out the merchandise. And one of your grandmother's class members, Vera, returned."

"That's good news."

"Yes, nice for business…until your friend here commented on their hair color."

He could only imagine what the women thought. Ricky's long, shaggy hair needed a good washing. His clothes were dirty, too. His scraggly goatee needed a trim, and his arms, what you could see of them under the tattoos, were well muscled, making him look brawny and threatening.

But Daniel had sensed the hurt under the brashness. He didn't think Ricky meant anyone harm. "I'm sorry for the interruption, Lilly. I'll take it from here." He nodded at Ricky. "Go out there and help the guys with the ceiling tiles."

Apparently, she hadn't been placated. She shut the door after Ricky walked out and massaged her shoulder. "Vera said Ricky frightened her. An over-reaction, of course. But still, she is a new customer. I hope this arrangement is going to be positive for The Yarn Barn."

Her tension arced across the space and into *his* shoulders. "I'll make sure it is." If he could control construction noise and three teenage boys who tended to land in trouble every chance they got.

"You know, I don't mean to come down on your mentoring program," she said. "In one town we lived in, Jenna and I had some church folks help us."

Her words hit him like a punch to the solar plexus. Her childhood must've been bleak if a church stepped in for the kids.

She closed in on herself, wrapping her arms around her middle. "Maybe the boys and Vera will learn to tolerate each other."

Her kind smile reached across his desk, letting him know all was well. Reminding him of their closeness at the foot of the ladder yesterday, a closeness he shouldn't want so badly.

"Thanks for understanding. They're good kids. Trying to make a better life for themselves."

"I totally get that." She walked out of his office and called, "Ricky, for what it's worth, that one woman's hair *is* blue. But I'd suggest a tighter filter on your thoughts."

Ricky's quiet chuckle trickled into Daniel's office.

He sucked in a deep breath, blew it out with a loud puff. Time to forget about a certain pair of hazel eyes and get back to work. Looked as if he'd be there through the night priming the walls. Saturday morning, he'd have to make a decision about whether to delay the move to the basement and hold the service back at Frank's.

## Chapter Five

By closing time on Saturday, battling the day-long desire to check on Daniel had left Lilly drained.

His car had been in the parking lot since Lilly had arrived that morning at seven-thirty. Since then she'd wanted to go to the basement, talk with him, see how he was doing. See how many volunteers showed up. See if he'd have to postpone the move.

She'd even battled asking if they needed help. But she was supposed to be focused on growing the yarn shop, not building a church. Especially if that church's pastor was Daniel.

The man held a powerful attraction. Charming, funny, smart. But she'd fallen for those qualities before with her ex-fiancé, Clint, and knew better.

*Daniel is much more than Clint could ever hope to be. He's kind, giving, patient....*

She imprisoned her wandering thoughts and sent Jenna home early. That was a sure way to conquer her urges once and for all, forcing her to remain upstairs, minding her own business.

Once she locked up for the night, though, she decided she had to know how Daniel was faring. Her recent reconnaissance mission revealed his was the only other car still in the lot. He had no assistance at the moment.

She had to go check on him. Any human being with a shred of concern would.

She would not flirt. She would not lean in. This was strictly a business concern. The man was renovating their building, after all.

She found him talking on his cell phone, sitting on a brand-new folding chair. He looked worn-out, with paint splattered in his hair and on his clothes—the same ones he'd worn yesterday.

He motioned for her to wait. "I'm fine. God will work it out, even if we finish after everyone gets here tomorrow." He squinted as if his eyes burned while he wrapped up the conversation and put the phone in his pocket.

"Did you work through the night last night?"

"Yep. Got the walls primed. Put on one coat of paint today. The final coat will have to be done next week."

She glanced around at the amazing amount of work they'd accomplished. The new ceiling made the room feel much more homey and muted the echo. "Everything looks great."

"Yep. With a good bit of help. How's the paint odor?"

"Not too bad since you have the door open. So you're meeting here tomorrow?"

He stood and turned, taking in all the changes around him. "Yes."

He still didn't have a place for people to sit. "What about the tables and chairs?"

"In boxes that I plan to open tonight. And if I have time, I'll run over to Frank's and move everything from my office."

"By yourself?"

"Yeah. That was Ned on the phone. The flu's going around the station. He's filling in again for a sick firefighter."

"I can help."

He seemed as surprised as she felt. All day long she'd held back. Had done very well at minding her own business. And now, with three careless words, she'd committed herself to a whole evening around the handsome preacher.

What on earth was she thinking?

His weary-yet-no-less-appealing grin made her stomach tie into a mishmash of pain…and excited nerves.

"You just surprised yourself, didn't you?" he asked.

"You're kind of scary, you know it?"

He shrugged. "I read people pretty well."

His face turned serious, and his normally confident, almost-cocky expression turned to one of doubt. He gave a little laugh. "I'm sure Jenna's expecting you. You can back out on that offer."

Hadn't he said she was good at jumping into action when needed?

Like now. Or else he'd be up all night again. And how could he preach when he'd been awake for forty-eight hours straight?

Not that the quality of his preaching mattered to her—it wasn't as if she planned to attend the service.

One glance at his tired eyes and she knew she wouldn't take the escape he'd offered. "Jenna doesn't need me. And y—this room does." She held her arms out to her sides. "So...tell me what to do."

Obviously relieved, his blue eyes brightened. He started to say something but stopped. Then he grabbed a box. "Let's set up these tables and chairs. And then maybe you can help me move my office. If you're game for all that?"

He looked unsure, which, for some reason, made her chest ache.

"Let's do it."

She called Jenna to let her know she'd be home a little late. They spent the next couple hours cleaning the construction mess, ripping open boxes and setting up large round tables and folding chairs. Nice chairs, unlike her ramshackle ones that were older than the ark.

"Oh, don't open those chair boxes over there." He pointed to a stack near the stairs. "They're extras I plan to return."

She looked around at all they'd finished. "This is a nice setup. I like that you sit around tables. Feels kind of homey."

"Those church folks you mentioned the other day...what did they do for you and Jenna?" he asked as if it were nothing. As if digging into someone's past was normal for him.

Of course, it probably was. Maybe she could trust him with some of her baggage. Her heart stuttered. *Might be nice to share it with someone.*

She pulled out a chair, and he joined her. One look into his sympathetic eyes reminded her she didn't see him as a pastor anymore. She was starting to see him as...more.

"They picked us up in a church van each Sunday and took us to Sunday school. They gave us groceries because Mom's paychecks often didn't stretch far enough."

He leaned forward and put a hand on her knee, a gesture of comfort that seemed automatic. "Man, Lilly. I'm sorry. I didn't realize it was that bad."

"Mom worked hard, but she was bitter about being the only one with a steady income while Dad chased his schemes. They ended up divorcing later, and Jenna and I became nothing more than pawns in court battles as they lashed out at each other."

He ran a hand through his hair, and the paint-encrusted ends stood straight up.

She laughed, smoothed them down. Then, embarrassed, stuffed her hands into her pockets. "It'll take forever to get that paint out."

He slapped his knees. Stood. "Well, it's late. You should probably get home to Jenna."

His dismissal hit like salt on a wound. She stood, ran her palms over the thighs of her khakis. Had she scared him off with her pathetic life story? The thought made her want to cry. "I can keep going."

He gazed into her eyes. Took a step closer, sending her stomach on a mad dash. "Are you sure?"

Sure of what? That she wanted to know him better? Wanted him to accept her for who she was, even though they would both eventually leave?

"I promised to help. I'll finish the job," she said, businesslike, certain. When in reality her insides felt like jelly.

He snapped into motion. Strode across the room and dug into a cooler. Tossed her a bottle of water, followed by a pack of peanut butter crackers. "Can't have you swooning on me."

How ironic.

They drove across town to Frank's. He didn't try to make conversation. Was probably too exhausted, or didn't want to listen to another sob story. She stared out the window at the beautifully lit courthouse. At the shadowed, barren winter tree line in the distance, the starkness of it calling to her as a kindred spirit.

"This won't take long. I've already packed." He hopped out and led her inside. They managed to load everything in less than a half hour. By the time they returned to The Yarn Barn, it was after ten o'clock. Lilly wasn't surprised when her cell phone rang, showing Jenna's home number on the display.

"Hey. I'm almost done," she answered. "Helping Daniel move his office stuff into the basement."

"Uh-huh." Jenna's tone implied she didn't believe a word.

"I am," she said firmly, her gaze darting to see if he was listening. As he carried a box inside, she stepped beside the open trunk of his car. "He was up all last night and looked like he was about to drop. So I stayed to help him finish."

"I'm not judging. Just be careful."

"Careful? Jenna, your mind is going way off base. I'll be home soon. We only have a few boxes to unload." She ended the call before Jenna could voice more of her out-there notions.

Daniel strode outside and propped his arm on the trunk, his broad shoulders blocking out the light from the church entrance. "I can get the last of it. Go on home to your family."

Cold wind sent a chill through her. She pushed her hair behind her ears as she reached for a box. "No, I'm good." Since he was so tired, he hadn't had his charmer persona so firmly in place that night. He'd acted more real, vulnerable. She wasn't ready yet to leave that behind.

He put a hand on her arm to stop her. "I'll get the books. They're too heavy."

Grabbing her hair into a bundle to keep it out of her face, she looked up at him, laughed. "The boxes are practically all books. Doesn't leave much for me to do."

"I've always devoured books—fiction, nonfiction."

"Escapism?" she dared ask.

With his hands in his pockets, he shrugged. "Maybe. I started reading a lot about the time my mom died."

"How old were you?"

"Eight." He raised his eyes to the sky. "Orion," he said as he pointed out the group of stars. Checking out the constellations. Avoiding talking about his past.

"How did she die?"

"Cancer."

Her heart ached for him. "Must've been difficult for you and your dad, with you so young."

"Yeah." His shoulders tensed, and then he snatched a box of books from the trunk as if it didn't weigh a thing and walked away. She picked up a lightweight box of office supplies and followed him inside. When she got to his office, she found him stacking books on his newly built shelf.

"I'm sorry if I pushed," she said.

"No. It's okay."

When he turned around in the small office, they were standing nearly toe-to-toe. He stared down into her eyes. "My dad wasn't able to be there for me. He was too deep in his own grief."

"Tough on a boy who needed his dad." She wanted to reach out to him. To comfort. But she didn't dare. She sensed the admission was a big moment for him. He might shut down if she touched him.

He took one step closer, so close she could see the ring of dark blue around his bright blue irises. "Thank you for understanding that."

The air stilled as they stared at each other, but it also pulsed with energy, energy that made her heart race and breathing difficult. As he leaned closer, the scent of winter air and man invading her senses, she held her breath.

Was he going to kiss her?

Her eyes fluttered closed. Yes, he was going to kiss her.

She sucked in a breath, and the intake of oxygen served to clear her head. Sanity snapped her eyes wide-open. What on earth was she doing? She wanted too much—love, trust, total commitment, security, permanence—and Daniel couldn't give all that.

"I better go," she said, his lips so close she could feel their warmth. The words stopped his forward motion, shattering the connection. A close call.

Daniel tensed and stepped away. "Yes. Good idea." He turned to his shelf and jammed another book into an empty spot with more force than necessary. "I appreciate the work you did. See you tomorrow."

Not if she could help it. She'd gotten the last of her aunt's belongings out of the basement yesterday. The space was all Daniel's now. She had no reason to travel those stairs again.

No, he wouldn't see her tomorrow—not for the worship service, not socially.

She'd nearly fallen into his arms like some kind of weak, dreamy fool. She wouldn't put herself in that position again.

What if Lilly didn't show for the first service in their new church location because of his actions the night before? Running a hand over his jaw, Daniel tried to push Lilly out of his mind to prepare, but his conscience drew his thoughts right back to her. He'd let her kindness suck him in. Had let his attraction to her get the best of him. How could he have leaned in like that, ready to kiss a woman who had trust issues—a woman he had no intention of starting a relationship with?

He needed to explain himself to her. If he could figure it out himself.

When he walked out of his new office, he ran into his grandmother and dad. "What a nice surprise."

"We wanted to see your new space and support you on your first Sunday here," Gran said. "It looks like a whole new place!"

"It's awfully humid down here," Blake said in his usual disapproving tone.

Too tired to deal with his dad's negativity, he

didn't even try to hold back a frustrated sigh. "I had to leave the door open because of traces of paint fumes. Just turned on the dehumidifiers a little while ago."

With a deep breath and quick prayer for patience, he turned to his grandmother. "I appreciate you both coming."

"We told Phil we'd be worshipping here today. He sends his thanks for working with his nephew."

"I hope it's helping." Phil might not be so appreciative if Daniel ended up reporting Ricky for being late on Friday. He needed to make a decision about whether to talk to Ricky's caseworker on Monday. Maybe he'd been telling the truth about trying to find the church location. Maybe they needed to give him the benefit of the doubt.

Like Daniel hoped Lilly would give him the benefit of the doubt.

As he placed his notes on a front table, he searched for Parker, Ian and Ricky. Not one of the teens had arrived. He made his way around the room welcoming everyone to their new church home, hoping the teens would show. Parker had only come once. The others claimed excuses each week. But he'd hoped assisting with the renovation might generate interest. He wouldn't give up.

Clusters of people stood around talking. He hadn't spotted Lilly, even though her car had been in the lot that morning.

He stepped into his office, pulled out his cell

phone and typed a text message. Sorry about last night. Was tired. Hope you and Jenna will come today. After wavering for a split second, he hit the send button.

Sending a text wasn't the perfect way to deal with the situation, but it was the best he could do with Lilly hiding out somewhere and the service about to start.

As much as he'd told himself to avoid her, he'd nearly dived in headfirst last night. If she hadn't come to her senses, he would have kissed her.

Lilly Barnes kept him awake at night, had him tied in knots. For what? A woman who put up walls faster than a defensive line. A woman who wasn't right for him. A woman who needed stability his life's calling wouldn't offer.

"Daniel," Frank's voice boomed. "We're waiting on you."

He'd have to do a better job protecting himself. He couldn't afford to fall for someone like Lilly.

Lilly couldn't resist.

She set aside her bookkeeping and stepped quietly across the yarn shop floor toward the basement door. She didn't dare attend the service. Especially not without Jenna, who'd elected to stay home since Ned was working and wouldn't be there. She'd claimed the tears at the previous service had been over her marriage falling apart, but Lilly couldn't help wondering if it was more. If maybe Jenna was afraid to come back.

Lilly's curiosity over the service wouldn't let up. She wanted to listen to the comments, to discover how the church members responded to their first Sunday at the new site.

She'd helped Daniel set up, so naturally, she'd be interested.

As she neared the door to the basement, she looked once again at the new chairs in the gathering area....

New nicely padded folding chairs.

Exactly like the ones downstairs.

A gift from the church? From Daniel? Yes, probably a gift from Daniel—a peace offering after he'd nearly put a move on her last night. Embarrassment over his apologetic text stung her cheeks.

The seats would make her class members more comfortable. But should she keep them?

The keyboard downstairs started playing, and once again, curiosity got the best of her. She slipped open the door as hands clapped to the beat and voices rose in song. She took a step down. Someone made a bumping sound near the bottom of the stairs and drove her back inside the shop, where she quickly shut the door. She wouldn't risk getting caught sneaking around.

As she headed to grab her purse to leave, she glanced once more at Daniel's message. He said he'd been tired. Was he offering that as an excuse for the near kiss?

*Sorry I leaned in and nearly planted my lips on yours. I was just tired. Not thinking straight. Would never have done it if I weren't sleep deprived.*

Yeah, that's probably what he meant by his cryptic message.

Her stomach quivered as she recalled his closeness, the blue of his eyes, the curve of his lips, the day's growth of beard—stubble a shade deeper than his dark golden blond hair.

A dumb move on her part to stand there waiting for the near kiss. Like a deer in headlights—except her eyes fell closed as if she was foolish enough to fall at his feet.

She jabbed at the button to delete the offending text and jammed her phone into her purse. Was she such a bad catch that he wouldn't even want to kiss her while in his right mind?

Embarrassment burned her face as tears stung her eyes. She had to get out of here.

She slung her purse over her shoulder and exited the shop. As she unlocked her car, leaves rustled nearby. She gasped and jerked around.

"Hey, Lilly." Ricky Hartley stood on the sidewalk wearing raggedy jeans and a thin nylon jacket—too thin for the cold winter morning. "Skipping out on church?" he said with a smirk.

She quickly blinked away the tears and squared her shoulders against the teen towering over her. "I wasn't here for the service—I came in to do some work." She nodded toward the side of the building. "They just started, if you want to go in."

His eyes narrowed as he examined her. Did she have mascara under her eyes?

"Nah. I was passing by. You okay?"

Yeah, right. He happened to be driving toward Appleton and parked and got out of his vehicle. "I'm fine. I imagine Daniel is hoping you'll show. Go on inside."

Panic flitted across his face before he fortified himself with the tough-guy exterior. "My uncle told me I had to come. I figure he's going to call Daniel to see if I showed, and might call my caseworker if I don't. I don't need *her* on my back, too."

Trying to make an excuse for showing up.

*Like me?* Her chest tightened. She hadn't needed to come to work today. The books would have kept until Monday.

He picked up a rock and tossed it far into the woods that surrounded the shop. "I've got too many people tellin' me what to do."

Poor Ricky. If he were truly a troublemaker, he wouldn't care what his uncle or his caseworker thought. "I suggest you head down there and prove to your uncle he can trust you."

His eyes flashed. "You think I care if he trusts me? He's not my dad, even if he tries to act like it."

"Where is your dad?" She asked it quietly, hoping not to push him away.

Ricky shoved his hands in his jeans pockets and kicked at a pile of leaves. If he didn't have the scraggly goatee, he'd look like a kid goofing around in the yard.

"Never knew my dad. I doubt my mom's even sure who he is."

His words slammed into her. "I'm sorry. That must be tough."

He shrugged.

"Do you live with your mom?"

Anger simmered in his eyes. "She took off who-knows-where with her boyfriend after we got kicked out of our apartment."

Lilly nearly groaned out loud. "Oh, man. I know about getting evicted."

His gaze met hers, darted away. "For real?"

"Happened when I was about seven. Again at thirteen." Memories of the humiliation and fear scalded her face. "So where do you stay now?"

"At a friend's house."

"I see."

"I'm an adult, you know. Almost eighteen. This court-ordered stuff, and Phil trying to get guardianship, is a joke."

The kid was hurting. And she knew from personal experience that he wouldn't head toward help on his own. He'd thrown up barriers that would stay in place unless someone forced him to engage with the people trying to support him.

"Come on." She nodded toward the side of the

building. "I didn't want to go by myself since my sister didn't come. If you'll go with me, I won't feel so conspicuous."

He studied her, as if doubting her sincerity. When she didn't flinch, his lip twitched. "So you *were* sneaking out."

Apparently, he recognized a kindred spirit when he saw one, because he turned and headed toward the church entrance without waiting to see if she followed.

Against her better judgment, she did.

## Chapter Six

Being around Ned always made Daniel think of Lilly. Although he didn't require reminding since she seemed to stay lodged in his mind.

She'd come to the worship service yesterday, had even brought Ricky.

But she'd avoided him. Hadn't said one word to him. And had hightailed it out of there as soon as they said the final *amen*.

Daniel hefted the last of the broken-down cardboard boxes from the basement of The Yarn Barn and took them outside to the bed of Ned's truck. "Thanks for hauling these off for recycling."

Ned climbed into the cab and rolled down his window. He gave the key a twist, and the engine growled to life. He smiled at Daniel, but it seemed strained. He hadn't been himself since he had left Jenna. He stayed active at church and work, but his eyes had lost their spark.

"So, Daniel, except for another coat of paint, the move from Frank's is done. What next?"

"Keep doing ministry." Daniel had been thinking along the same lines all morning. One big item checked off his to-do list—but there was still plenty on it. "Hey, that reminds me. The new food pantry is about to open in Appleton. The Smiths donated the materials for shelving for food storage. Could you get someone to help you hang it?"

"I'll do it later this week."

"Thanks. I've also been toying with an idea…."

"Nope. Can't do it." He laughed. "Just jokin'. What is it?"

"When I visited Cricket today, Mrs. Quincy confirmed the need for a support group for teen girls. She's even willing to help fund activities for the meetings."

"Sounds like a good plan. What kind of activity did you have in mind?"

"That's the big question." He tightened a rope holding the tarp. "I've been thinking these girls might like to learn to knit. And since you have some connections at the yarn shop…"

Ned's face turned red. "I'm not exactly in the good graces of the Barnes sisters right now."

Daniel winced. "Sorry. I'd hoped it might be a way to get you and Jenna talking."

He shook his head. "We could use your continued prayers."

"You've got it." He reached out and shook Ned's hand. "Thanks again for hauling the boxes."

A little life flashed in his sad eyes. "Hey, you and Lilly seemed close at lunch over at Frank's last week. Why not talk to her?"

They'd been a little *too* close lately. "Not sure about that...."

"Lilly's practical and all business. If hosting the girls will help the yarn shop in some way, I think she'll go for it. Besides, she's got a good heart, especially when it comes to people down on their luck."

"Thanks for the tip." He waved and walked inside.

Surely he could stay focused on business for five minutes, could go talk to her about a worthy project without wanting to run his fingers through her hair or to kiss her.

He would stay focused on touting what the support group could do for The Yarn Barn's business, and what a difference it could make to the girls. Before he could overthink his plan, he headed upstairs.

Lilly had a customer and looked startled that the basement door had opened. "Can I help you, Daniel?" she asked. She sounded neutral, so much so that he wondered if she'd received his apology text.

"I'll wait here until you're done." He stepped over to the gathering area and sat in one of the nice new chairs. Rather than send several extra chairs back to the store, he'd bought them for her, wanting to do something since she'd helped him finish the place Saturday night.

Once her customer checked out with what looked to be a large bag of stuff, she joined him. "What's up?"

He nodded toward the front door. "A big sale?"

"Very big." Her neutral expression warmed.

"That's fantastic."

"Now, if we could get more people in here to do the same, we'd be in good shape."

The perfect lead-in. "I have an idea for how we can bring some new business your way." Proud of himself for staying on task, he motioned for her to have a seat beside him.

She hesitated, concern drawing together her brows. Worried that he might act like he had on Saturday night?

She joined him, anyway. "By the way, I, uh, didn't get a chance to speak with you yesterday. Thank you for the chairs. Is this a gift from the church?"

Her hopeful expression indicated she wanted them to be from the congregation.

"No. From me. A thank-you for your work. For letting us share your building."

Her obvious disappointment made him tense up. "Was I presumptuous?"

"Of course not. They'll be great for class attendees. I appreciate the generous gift."

But apparently, he'd made some sort of blunder. He wanted to reach out and smooth the worry line from between her eyes. To try to fix what he'd messed up.

*Are you kidding, Foreman. What's to fix? There isn't any kind of relationship, and can't be.*

*Focus.* "The idea I mentioned…? This would generate income for you as well as help others. Teenage girls."

"Is this the idea you were scribbling notes about at Frank's last Sunday?"

Her tone had an edge to it. "Did that offend you somehow?"

She crossed her arms tightly in front of her chest as if holding herself together. "I'm sorry. I've just seen a lot of ideas fail."

"Yours…or your dad's?"

She popped up out of the chair. Fiddled with the coffeepot. "Guess." She shook her head, disgusted. "Dad always jotted ideas on notes on every surface of the room, like your sticky notes. They usually entailed a move somewhere after he'd been fired."

Returning to his side, she sat primly on the edge of her chair, straight as a razor in her perfectly pressed khaki slacks and expensive-looking sweater. Why had he never noticed before how she always dressed to the T? He didn't think he'd ever seen her wear jeans.

"I'm not your dad," he said.

"You're an ideas man, planning to start things and then moving on. That's my dad all over again."

"No, I've tried to tell you, I plan to stick around until everything is secure and going well. I'm not leaving before the church is ready or before I feel God leading me elsewhere."

"So when it's time, does God give you marching papers?"

"Not exactly." If only it were that easy. He'd felt God nudge him along certain paths—like his change of careers. But he sometimes doubted his ability to discern between God's will and his own selfish desires. Like with Lilly.

"I can't really explain it," he said. "I feel nudges while I'm praying and reading the Bible. Sometimes God puts certain people, certain Scriptures in my path. Or guides me by using others who share their wisdom with me. Sometimes He has to be more direct, slamming doors in my face."

"So this job in South Georgia, this new church you'll start...you feel God wants you to go there?"

"I..." He hesitated. Something held him in check. Was this one of those nudges? *Lord?*

She tilted her head, questioning, waiting for him his answer.

This sudden doubt left him shaken. "I've felt Him leading me that way for the last few weeks. I spoke with church leaders there this morning, told them we have one more big project to accomplish here."

"The project you came to talk to me about?"

"Actually, no. The food pantry in Appleton. I came to tell you about a support group for girls. To help Cricket and others."

"And what you want me to do is...?"

"I'd love for you to host gatherings here. I can find someone to lead the group. The girls could learn to knit, and donations would fund the supplies. A win-win for your shop and for the girls."

Her eyes widened. "Wait a minute. Just because I came on Sunday—and only to get Ricky through the door, I might add—doesn't mean I'm going to get involved." She looked almost panicky.

"By the way, thanks for bringing Ricky yesterday."

Her cheeks pinkened, thawing her cool demeanor a little. "No big deal. I ran into him outside. He was going to leave, too proud to attend simply because his uncle would be checking up on him. So I asked him to come with me so I wouldn't feel out of place."

Pain squeezed at his chest. "You're a kind person, Lilly Barnes. Whether you'll admit it or not."

She looked away, and the pink in her cheeks deepened. "I totally understand teen angst. I knew he'd put up walls and wouldn't back down. So I offered him a way out...or maybe I should say a way in."

Once again, he envisioned her helping a group of high school girls, gathered around in a circle, knitting. "You're a natural at working with troubled teenagers. We could sure use your gifts here at the church. I think you'd be happy finding a church home."

With a shrug, she blew off his suggestion. "It might seem that way to you because churchgoing is something you're used to. Not everyone feels the need."

*Lord, help her to open up. To trust.* He rested his forearms on his thighs, leaning toward Lilly. He knew pain when he saw it. "Maybe not. But I hope you'll give it a try now, that you'll once again feel God in your life. He's still there, Lilly, loving you."

Tears filled her eyes. She blinked wildly and stood, avoiding eye contact. "I'm sure Jenna could use a break. She's in the back with Will."

Lilly took off like a dart. He followed her to the sales counter.

Jenna carried Will out of the back room. "Hello, Daniel."

Will turned and smiled when he saw Daniel. He reached out, nearly launching himself from his mother's arms.

He took the baby from across the counter. "Hey, buddy. Are you feeling a little overwhelmed by all this female crafty stuff?" He smiled at Lilly, who stood quietly behind the counter as if she'd still like to run into the back. She appeared to have a handle on the tears.

Will blew some saliva bubbles and giggled. Cute little guy. Daniel hoped to be blessed with kids someday himself.

"You should be honored, Daniel." Jenna wiped her son's chin. "He doesn't go to just anybody."

"Eeee," Will squealed as he kicked his feet over and over, like motioning Daniel to giddyap.

With a laugh, he said, "I think he associates me with pizza."

Lilly laughed at the two of them, which sent his insides into a jumble.

Back to the topic at hand. "Jenna, I was just telling Lilly about an opportunity to host a teen girls' support group here, teaching them to knit. And the church would buy any supplies with donations."

"I don't think it's something we'd be interested in," Lilly said.

"If it'll bring in some business, maybe we should consider it." Jenna's gaze landed on Lilly. "Something maybe you could have at least discussed with me first?"

"We're not equipped to handle troubled teens."

"I'd consider us experts. But you two work it out." Jenna reached for her son. "Come on, Will. Nap time."

After pulling at Daniel's lip with slobbery fingers, Will went to his mom.

Daniel opened his mouth to speak, but Lilly held up her hand to stop him.

"Save your breath," she said. "I'm not qualified to teach your teen girls—knitting or otherwise."

"I'm trying to help you build your business."

"Then give me the name of a company you'd recommend. You were right—the store needs more visible signage."

The admission seemed to pain her. When he

chuckled, her pretty hazel eyes flashed with humor, all her earlier emotions tightly under control.

"I'll run downstairs and look up the company. I think you'll see an immediate increase in business if people can find the place."

"That's what we need."

He winked at her on the way out the basement door. "I won't give up on having you host the group, though."

He was glad she'd accepted help in marketing her shop. But he was no closer to realizing his plan for the troubled girls. He'd have to petition the women of the church for a host for the group and hope someone would step forward.

Surely he would arrive any minute.

Lilly stood out front of the yarn shop, repeatedly checking her watch. He had said Wednesday at noon, hadn't he?

The man from the sign company had promised to install the permanent site sign. He would complete magnetic vehicle signs and portable yard signs to place around town by next week. But he was already an hour late.

Lilly tried to ignore the knot furling in her stomach. Why did she always fear the worst?

Her mother had called her a pessimist, but she refused to agree. She was simply a realist. And most often, people let you down.

*A watched pot never boils.* She went back inside,

reassuring herself that Daniel had recommended the company. The man would call or show up soon.

When the front bell rang, she raced to the entrance of the store.

"Hello, Lilly," said a fiftyish woman, a brunette with a cute bobbed cut whom she'd seen at the church services. A woman who'd acted friendly and welcoming and always looked happy.

"Hi…um…I'm sorry, but you'll have to remind me of your name."

"I wouldn't expect you to remember since you've been meeting so many new people," she said warmly and held out her hand. "I'm Belinda Hodges, and I'm so happy we're neighbors."

She paused while shaking. "Neighbors? You live near my sister?"

"No, I mean sharing the building. My husband and I have been members since the church started. I'm also one of the check signers along with Daniel and the treasurer. Since I practically live at the church…well, I feel like we're neighbors."

With her carefree laugh and dancing eyes, Belinda radiated joy. A joy that seemed to light her from inside. Lilly liked her immediately. "I'm glad you stopped by. What can I help you with today?"

"Actually, I'm here to ask you the same thing." She held open a tote bag and showed Lilly a stash of yarn. "I've heard through the grapevine, meaning Daniel, that you need to relearn how to knit. I'm offering my services."

Lilly rarely asked for help. But something about Belinda drew her...

"No pressure," the woman added. "I know how it is to get out of practice. I put away my yarn away for about twenty years before picking it back up to knit something for my new grandbaby. That was five years ago, and now I take my knitting with me everywhere I go." She leaned closer. "Even to church. But don't tell Daniel that's why I sit in the back."

Lilly laughed and directed Belinda to the gathering area. "Your secret is safe with me. And I really could use some help. I've been practicing, but I keep dropping stitches and having to pull it all out and start over."

"Grab your stuff and let me see what's going wrong."

"I'm glad you're here. I was killing time, waiting—impatiently, I might add—for the store's new sign to arrive."

After about thirty minutes with the expert, they'd picked out bamboo needles to help keep the yarn from slipping and had also changed Lilly to a different weight yarn for beginners.

"Much better! Look, I've knitted four whole rows without having to rip them out and start over."

"Call me anytime you get stuck and can't figure it out."

"Since we're neighbors and all." She smiled at her new friend, who returned the gesture with a pat on her arm.

Lilly shifted the tail of the yarn forward to attempt a row of the purl stitch.

"I see you bought some of the chairs like we have downstairs," Belinda said as she whipped out a row of her own.

"Daniel gave them to me."

"Oh?" The last was said softly.

She didn't dare look into Belinda's eyes in case the woman was trying to read her. No way could she hide the mixed feelings she'd been having for him.

"A thank-you gift," Lilly said.

"He told us how grateful he was that you helped him late into the night so we could move in as planned."

"The poor man was exhausted. It was the least I could do."

Lilly glanced at her watch for the first time in nearly an hour. Time to contact the sign company. She put away her knitting.

"Belinda, thank you so much for helping me. I got more done today than the last two weeks put together. And with much less frustration."

"You're welcome. I'd love to come work with you again."

Two friends getting together to knit and chat? She'd dreamed of that for her shop, but she'd never imagined herself in the scenario.

"I'd like that. I'm here most of the time, at least for now while I'm learning the business."

"Great! I'll come again later this week." She gathered her bag and left.

Lilly dialed the company and got a recording that the number had been disconnected. Her stomach dropped. Maybe she'd dialed incorrectly.

She tried again, double-checking the numbers, and got the same recording. When she opened the computer to search the website for a phone number change, she found the site had been removed.

She'd paid the man a deposit of half the total estimate. Several hundred dollars. Dollars she'd hated to part with but had hoped would be a good investment.

And she'd been ripped off.

Her stomach churned. Jenna would be furious. She hadn't wanted her to make the purchase.

She should probably let Daniel know, so he wouldn't recommend the company again.

She found him in his tiny closet-office. Files and notepads were scattered across his desk. He had a pen in hand but looked up when he sensed her standing there. As soon as he saw her, his thousand-watt smile emerged—something she might have been pleased about if she hadn't been so disappointed.

One good look at her, and his face fell. "What's wrong?"

"The sign guy ripped me off."

"What?" He stood and came around the desk.

"He never showed. His website's gone and his phone number is disconnected. I feel sure an email will bounce back, undeliverable."

The horrified look on Daniel's face almost made her wish she hadn't told him. He looked as sick as she felt.

"I'm sorry. I've used him before. Never would have expected this."

She shrugged. "Don't worry about it. It can't be helped."

As she turned to tromp back up the stairs, he stopped her. "This is my fault. I'll try to locate him to get you a reimbursement. If I can't find him, I'll pay you back whatever you lost."

"It's not your fault. I hired him." And without checking on him like Jenna had suggested. "I'll eat the cost of my mistake." She headed up the stairs.

"Lilly, wait." When he reached her, she was already several steps above him. "I'd really like to help."

If only she could lean on him. Allow herself to care for him. But trusting any man was hard enough. And he was definitely off-limits, a man who would move from church to church, following God's call.

She could never be happy uprooting every few months. "No, thanks. I'm fine on my own."

And wasn't that the story of her life? Always eating the cost of her mistakes.

Always alone.

Daniel had let Lilly down with his supposed marketing advice. Now Ricky hadn't shown up, which didn't say much for Daniel's ability to mentor troubled teens.

"Are you sure you two don't know where he is? I need you to be totally honest."

"I don't have a clue," Parker said, his blue eyes guileless.

Ian sat hunched over Daniel's laptop typing a paper for his lit class. "Don't know. Don't really care. He's a jerk."

Daniel had set up a study hall for the guys since all three had a bad habit of skipping school. Two of their teachers were willing to give them another chance and had sent over makeup assignments.

But Ricky hadn't shown.

"I didn't see him at school today, either," Parker said.

Daniel shut himself in his office. What else could he do to reach Ricky? Unfortunately, any progress they'd made would end up strained after he reported Ricky to his caseworker for being a no-show.

He pulled out his cell phone and dialed Phil.

"Hi, Daniel. What's up?"

"Ricky didn't show this afternoon. The other boys haven't seen him today and don't know anything."

"Let me call my wife and see if she knows anything. I'll call you right back."

He headed up the stairs to the yarn shop to see if Lilly knew anything about the boy's whereabouts. When he entered, he found Lilly and Jenna facing off behind the counter.

"Hi, ladies."

"What do you want?" Jenna snapped.

"I need to talk to Lilly, but I can come back."

Lilly held up her hand to stop him. "No, it's—"

"I think you've done enough talking with Lilly in that bogus sign company recommendation." Jenna glared at him, her bright green eyes flashing fury, and maybe a little hurt.

"Look, I'm really sorry about that. The marketing firm I worked for before attending seminary used them. So it had been a few years. I should have checked recent references."

"You better believe it," Jenna said. "I didn't want her to spend the money in the first place. But she trusted your judgment."

The barb landed as intended. The fact Lilly had trusted him made him feel even worse. "I'd like to repay whatever you lost."

"And I'd like to accept it. But Lilly refuses."

Lilly came from behind the counter. "Jenna, stop it. This is between you and me." She nodded toward the front door, motioning him to follow her outside.

"She's going to take the money out of her measly savings to cover the loss," Jenna called as he and Lilly stepped out the door.

"Ignore her. She's worried. And when she's worried, she lashes out." Lilly reached back and yanked the door shut. "Why did you need to see me?"

"Are you really using your savings?"

She crossed her arms in front of her, shielding

from the cold. And probably from him. "That's my business."

"It'll make me feel better if you let me cover it."

Her hazel eyes weren't flashing anger like her sister's. No, hers were tired but resolved. With one look he could tell she'd refuse to budge.

"I came to see if you'd heard from Ricky. He's a no-show today."

She shook her head and sighed. "Running into him on Sunday was a fluke."

Before he could finish filling her in on the situation, his cell phone rang. Phil. "Yeah, any news?"

"He skipped school today. And the friend he's been staying with said his duffel bag and some clothes are missing."

Daniel's heart sank. "So he's run away?"

"Looks like it. And he's got an eight-hour jump on us."

They had to try to find him. "We should split up. Where do you want me to start looking?"

"I'll check with his mother. You look locally." Once Phil gave a list of possible places to search, they hung up.

Lilly's face scrunched in concern. "Ricky's run off?"

"Yeah. I need to take the other boys home so I can help look for him."

"You want me to run them home for you?"

What he really wanted, he had no right to ask. But maybe she and Ricky had connected. It couldn't hurt to try. "I'd rather you come with me. You might be able to reach Ricky when no one else can."

"Assuming you find him."

He ground together his teeth. "We have to find him. I won't consider the alternative."

"Then let me ask Jenna to cover for me, and I'll go with you."

He couldn't remember when he'd been more relieved. Her offer pushed the sick feeling into submission.

He had an ally. They would find Ricky.

## Chapter Seven

Lilly ran inside to get her coat. "Jenna, can you cover the shop by yourself for a while?"

"You're not asking me so you can go somewhere with that man, are you?"

"I thought you liked Daniel. Why is he suddenly *that man?*"

Jenna looked away, but not before Lilly saw the hurt and anger. "We asked him to bring his church here to help us financially. And now it's cost us nothing but heartache and money."

Heartache? Something else was going on besides money woes. "I told you, I'm covering the loss. It won't hurt Aunt Talitha's business."

She bounced Will on her hip and stared at the computer.

"Jenna, what's wrong?"

"He's taking my husband away," she snapped.

"What in the world are you talking about?"

"I've been thinking a lot about it…" She set Will

in the playpen she'd moved to the store and handed him his stuffed dog. "My marriage problems started when Ned began going to that man's church," she said, her voice laced with uncharacteristic venom.

"Your marriage problems may be about a lot of things, but they aren't about Ned attending church. If anything, that should make him a better man and father."

"Since when did you start spouting the party line?"

When *had* she started to think that way? Once she'd attended services herself? "It's not like I'm one of them. But I've seen the good work they're doing. They wouldn't lead your husband away from his family."

"You know where he is right this minute? Putting up some stupid shelves for the food pantry when he has a broken kitchen cabinet that needs fixing at his own house."

"Come on, Jenna. Listen to yourself. That food pantry will feed hungry people."

"You're just saying that because you're interested in Daniel. I see the way you look at him."

The comment knocked her on her heels. Heat streaked from her chest to the tips of her ears. "Whoa! Back up a minute. I'm not interested in Daniel. I know better than to get involved with a man like him—a man who'll be moving on before long."

"Then why are you hanging around him, helping

him, asking me to cover for you while you go trotting off somewhere?"

She had the urge to hug her sister but kept her hands at her side. Neither of them were touchy-feely people. "Ricky Hartley, a troubled teen the church has been helping, ran away. And since, for whatever reason, Ricky talked to me on Sunday, Daniel thinks maybe I can convince him to come home."

Jenna didn't say a word, just paced behind the counter.

"So can you handle the shop for a while?"

"That means I'll probably have to close again by myself."

"Yes. Or you can close early if you feel you need to take Will home."

As if he'd heard his name, he started to whimper and fuss to get out of the playpen.

Jenna stepped around the counter and continued to pace in a larger area. "Maybe I can call Ned to help me."

Lilly picked up Will to soothe him and carried him to his mother. "If he's not working, I'm sure he'll be glad to."

As Jenna took her son, she looked at Lilly, almost guiltily. "I'm really not a bad person, you know. I want you to find the kid."

"I do know that. You and I tend to lash out when we're hurt or scared. I want to try to move beyond our past." And to move beyond Clint's betrayal.

Jenna sighed. "Go with Daniel. I'll call Ned."

The desperate look in Jenna's eyes made Lilly hug her sister. "I hope he comes, and that you get to talk."

Jenna held on tightly. "Me, too. Now go, before I change my mind." She pushed Lilly away and headed to the storeroom with her son.

Lilly grabbed a coat, her purse and a notepad, then joined Daniel, Parker and Ian at Daniel's car.

"What's the paper for?" Parker asked.

"You two are going to tell me all the places you think Ricky might have gone. And give me names and phone numbers of anyone he might've contacted."

Once the boys had given her all the information they could—which wasn't much, they drove Parker home. Then they headed to Ian's.

Ian said goodbye as he got out at a dilapidated, shacklike house.

"Where to first?" Daniel asked.

"I can't believe anyone could actually live there. Looks like it could fall down at any moment." Her heart hurt as she watched the boy walk inside. Trash littered the yard. A broken-out front window had been covered with a cardboard box. A scrawny dog barked at them from his short chain that had wrapped around a tree. All signs of neglect.

Ian probably wasn't treated any better.

Images of her and Jenna huddled up at night for warmth, their stomachs growling, played like a slide show through her mind.

"Rough family situation," Daniel said. He glanced her way. "You okay?"

"It hits a little too close to home."

His hands gripped and released the steering wheel. Then gripped again like he wished he could punish someone. Like he wished he could defend her. It made her nearly cry.

"Want to talk about it?" he asked.

She dragged herself away from the past and from Ian's dismal house. "No. We need to call the two possible friends Parker named."

They pulled into a nearby parking lot. Daniel hopped out to make one of the calls.

She had no luck with hers. When Daniel glanced inside, she shook her head.

He climbed back in. "Nothing. But Phil called. His sister hasn't seen or heard from Ricky. I told Phil we'd drop by the apartment complex where Ricky and his mom lived until they were evicted to see if he's taken up with any of his former neighbors."

They got back in the car and drove around downtown Corinthia looking for Ricky's ragtag red pickup truck. They didn't see it anywhere near the square, so they went two streets over to the ramshackle apartment complex. A pile of old, worn furniture was strewn haphazardly at the curb.

"You think that belongs to the Hartleys?" he asked.

She didn't want to know.

Ricky's truck wasn't anywhere in the parking lot,

so they stopped and got out of Daniel's car. The complex was small. Making the rounds didn't take long. No one had seen Ricky or his truck since they'd moved out weeks ago. As they exited the lot, a boy about middle school age waved at them.

Lilly rolled down her window.

The kid was clean-cut and dressed nicely. "Heard you're looking for Ricky."

"Yes. Have you seen him lately?"

"Yeah. He came by today looking for his dog."

Daniel leaned across Lilly. "His dog?"

"Yeah. They left it when they got kicked out. Heard him whistling for it today."

Once again, Lilly's heart ached for Ricky. Pets cost money. And they didn't handle moves well.

"Did he say where he was going?" Daniel asked.

"Nah. Said he was looking for his dog."

"Thanks." Daniel slid back over to his seat.

She started to roll up the window but paused halfway. "Did he find it?"

The boy's eyes grew sad. "I don't think so."

Something about the boy—his clothes so perfect—reminded her of herself after the humiliation over the dirty clothes incident. From that moment on, she'd sworn she'd never again look poor.

"What's your name?" she asked as he turned to walk away.

"Darren. But everyone calls me Dag."

"Well, Dag, Daniel, here, has an after-school program for boys. Have your mom or dad call the church and ask about it." She glanced at Daniel. "Do you have a business card?"

His eyes wide, he paused before quickly recovering and whipping one out of the glove box. He reached across her and handed it over.

"Cool." The boy's brown eyes brightened.

"Dag, I'd appreciate it if you'd call that number if you see Ricky again. Hope to see you around."

He nodded, then walked back toward the apartments.

"So he came for his dog," Lilly said.

"I don't know if that's good or bad."

They sat in silence for a few minutes, Daniel bowing his head to pray, lips moving quietly, his words a mere whisper. Lilly turned away and stared out the window, hoping daylight would hold out.

Her mind kept going back to the previous Sunday and replaying it in her head. Then she replayed the day Ricky offended Vera and the ladies. "You know, Daniel, both times when Ricky was supposed to show up for his court-ordered community service, he was outside avoiding going in."

His intense sky-blue eyes bore into hers. "Surely not."

"Could be. Let's go look around The Yarn Barn."

They headed back to the shop. No sign of Ricky's truck in the parking lot. But then, he wasn't stupid. If he didn't want to be found, he could hide it anywhere.

A quick search around the building didn't yield any clues.

"You don't think he'd be in the woods do you?" Daniel asked.

In the winter? Not something she would ever do. But Ricky could feel desperate to get away from everyone. "Let's check."

They didn't have to go far before they found a pup tent set up in a small clearing under a pine tree. She pointed.

Daniel's head fell back in relief so palpable it made Lilly's eyes sting. He really cared for these kids, for the people he pastored. Even though he knew he'd be leaving, he'd invested himself in the community.

She imagined once he found the right woman, he'd give himself wholly to her, as well.

He put his arm around her shoulders and gave a gentle squeeze. "Nice work," he whispered. Then he approached the tent. "Ricky? You in there?"

A loud bark rang out, followed by a deep, menacing growl. Lilly nearly ran the other direction, but then she realized the dog was zipped inside.

Ricky had found his dog.

"Go away," Ricky shouted through the closed flap.

"We need to talk."

"How'd you find me?"

Daniel glanced at Lilly. "Why didn't you show up today?"

"I'm ready to be on my own. Plan to keep to myself until my birthday. Now leave me alone."

The dog growled again.

Daniel leaned close to Lilly's ear. "Can you try? He may talk to you."

He trusted her in this crazy situation? Swallowing back trepidation, she stepped toward the tent. "Ricky, it's Lilly."

"Aah, man. Why are you here?"

"I care what happens to you."

He sighed behind the nylon barrier. "I guess I was wrong about you. If you really understood, you'd let me go. Only nine more months, and I'll be eighteen."

"A lot can happen in nine months," she said.

Ricky gave an ironic laugh, but the laugh turned into something else entirely. Something that sounded, oddly, like the combination of a cry and groan.

"You okay, Ricky?" Daniel asked.

"Go away, man." He sniffed.

Daniel's mouth drew into a narrow line. He stepped closer to the tent and put out his hand, ready to reach for the zipper. "Will you let Lilly in to talk?"

Slowly, the zipper opened. A defeated Ricky walked out.

Alarm shot through Lilly at the grief-stricken look on his face.

"Yeah, I'll talk to Lilly."

A big dog tore out of the tent and ran straight at Lilly. She screamed as Daniel shoved her behind him.

Then she realized the dog's tail was wagging. He circled them, thumping her with his wriggling rear end, sniffing both her and Daniel. The vicious-sounding attack dog was actually an overly friendly yellow lab mix.

When Lilly realized Daniel still kept himself between her and the dog, something hard inside her softened, warmed. No one had ever defended her against a threat. Tears welled. "Thanks, Daniel."

Humor lit his eyes. "Killer puppy."

"I appreciate it." She rubbed the pup's ears. "Nice dog, Ricky. What's his name?"

"Quincy."

Daniel tensed. "Interesting name for a dog." His eyes narrowed, and he stared at Ricky as if searching, waiting.

Lilly couldn't figure out where Daniel's suspicion stemmed from.

Ricky challenged Daniel with squared shoulders and clenched fists. "Go ahead. Ask me."

Daniel's expression didn't change. He looked calm, but she recognized the tension coiled in his body. "How'd your pup get that name?"

"After my ex-girlfriend. Cricket Quincy."

Girlfriend? Lilly's heart raced. Could it be?

"Are you the father of her baby?" Daniel asked.

Ricky's shoulders heaved, but he maintained control. "I want to talk to Lilly. I trust her."

*No, no, no! Don't trust me. Trust Daniel. He's the one who can help you.* She screamed the words in her head but didn't utter a sound.

"Let's all three talk," Daniel suggested. "We'll

go back to the church or the yarn shop. Wherever you want to go."

"I don't want to go to Phil and Marla's."

"We won't make you," Lilly said, although she had no idea why she, an outsider, was stepping into this complicated scene. She squatted down and rubbed Quincy's ears.

As she avoided a bath from the dog's tongue, she noticed Ricky's defensive stance had softened while watching her with Quincy. Maybe the dog was the way to break down the boy's barriers.

"Let's go talk somewhere Ricky can take Quincy. We can go to my house."

Daniel glanced at her, questioning. Then he nodded. "Good idea."

She didn't give Ricky a chance to refuse. "Come on. Daniel can drive. He won't mind a little fur in his car when it's on someone so adorable." She winked at Daniel as she wrapped her arm around the puppy's warm neck.

"You promise you won't call my uncle?"

"We need to let him know you're safe," she said. "But we won't send you over there until you're ready."

He nodded and seemed to believe her, but then he turned a skeptical eye toward Daniel. "I need to hear you promise."

"I'll leave the decision to Lilly. This time."

Lilly wanted to run. To ignore the possibility this kid was responsible for Cricket's pregnancy.

To ignore the fact he trusted her and looked to her for guidance. She wanted to head back to the shop, preferring the ups and downs of the yarn business to this. But she couldn't. Whether she liked it or not, she was now involved in Ricky's life.

And thus, in Daniel's.

Daniel watched the scene unfold before him, trying to stay out of it so as not to inhibit Ricky—who didn't yet trust him for some reason.

Lilly had been amazing. She'd gotten past Ricky's defenses in no time.

*Ricky's the father of Cricket's baby.*

Daniel still couldn't wrap his mind around it.

Ricky swiped at tears as if wanting to punish himself for his weakness, furious at his show of emotion. "I can't step forward. She said her parents would kill her for going out with me after they'd forbidden it. How do you think that makes me feel, when all I want—" He heaved a shaky breath. "I want to know my son."

The painful admission sent him into shuddering sobs.

Lilly glanced over at Daniel, alarmed. She patted Ricky's shoulder. When the boy fell against her, she only hesitated for a moment before awkwardly wrapping her arms around him, holding him while he let go of the pain.

When his crying lessened, he pulled away, sniffing. Scrubbed at his eyes.

Lilly squeezed his shoulder. "I understand Cricket's fear over her parents' reaction. But a baby changes the game."

"Yeah." He jumped up and paced across the small living room of Jenna and Ned's home. The floor was scattered with baby equipment. He stopped and stared at a musical toy, rubbed his fingers over it. "A baby changes everything."

Daniel had to weigh in at some point. Maybe Ricky was ready to listen. "You need to step up and take responsibility."

His shoulders slumped. "Don't you think I know that? How can I when she told me to forget about her?"

Lilly glanced Daniel's way and then said, "Cricket's been having a hard time."

"I heard the rumors. She won't answer my calls." He ran a hand through his scraggly hair. "What else can I do?"

With a hand on his arm, Lilly said, "You probably need to go through her parents, to make sure it's okay to talk with her."

"Do you love her?" Daniel asked.

He nodded and swallowed back a sob.

"Do you think she loves you?"

Another nod.

"Can I give you my suggestion?" He waited, unsure whether the kid would be willing to listen.

"You can trust Daniel," Lilly urged.

With a sniff and another swipe at his eyes, Ricky straightened. "Okay."

"Go talk to your aunt and uncle. Tell them what's going on. Maybe they'll approach Cricket's parents and set up a meeting. The six of you could talk."

Red streaked across Ricky's cheeks, and he looked ready to shoot down the idea.

"That's a great idea, Daniel," Lilly interjected before he could refuse.

The boy looked at her for a minute, and she smiled at him, encouraging.

"Don't you think we've been trying to figure out what to do? Cricket finally just shut me out." He held his head between his hands. "Man, I'm so messed up."

Lilly leaned in front of him, forcing him to look her in the eye. "Let the adults help you and Cricket decide the best course of action."

His hands flopped to his sides. "I guess that's my only choice at this point. I just have a part-time job, and I'm barely passing in school."

"It's never too late to change," Daniel said. "Time to step up and be the man—the father—God wants you to be." A risky comment, but one he felt he had to make.

Ricky nodded, and maybe stood a little taller.

"Come on. Let's take you home," Lilly said.

Ricky didn't argue about the definition of home. He simply started toward the door. "Oh, wait. My uncle said no dogs in their house, since my aunt's allergic."

No wonder the poor kid hadn't wanted to move in with his aunt and uncle. He'd had to leave part of his family behind, and his own mother had left the dog to wander the neighborhood.

Daniel looked at Lilly, who was crouched beside Quincy, rubbing his chin. Her eyes widened. "Don't look at me."

He loved seeing her loosen up, be affectionate. "You and the dog have already bonded."

Ricky sniffed. "He does seem to like you, Lilly. And it'll only be temporary, until I can get a place of my own or talk my aunt into letting me keep him."

"I don't know…" she said.

"I'll buy the dog food and a nice, warm bed," Daniel added.

She laughed. "Another bribe?"

"Incentive."

"Oh…okay. The backyard is fenced in. Unless Jenna objects, I think he'll be fine out there for a day or two."

Ricky's breath rushed out. "Good. At least that's taken care of. Now I have to face telling Uncle Phil and Aunt Marla what a mess I've made of my life."

Daniel clapped him on the back. "I'll be praying for you."

Lilly left Jenna a note to let her know what was going on, telling her to call if she had any objections.

Once they'd set up the puppy in the backyard with some shelter under the porch and a bowl of water, they piled into Daniel's car and drove to the Hartleys'. The pastor and his wife hugged their nephew profusely and thanked them for bringing him home. Daniel felt sure they'd left Ricky in good hands.

Then they drove to the store, and he bought dog food and a bed as promised. He felt a sense of accomplishment. Like they'd done something good. Together.

"You ever had a pet?" he asked on the way back to Jenna's.

She stared out the passenger window into the darkness. "No. We weren't allowed. Made moving easier."

Hearing the pain behind the words, he winced. "I had a dog when I was young, a big shaggy mutt of unknown origin." He shook his head, remembering Daisy's unconditional love. "But once she died, Dad wouldn't let me get another."

She reached out and touched his arm, her eyes sad. "I'm sorry. Did you ever get a dog after you left home?"

"Nope. Too busy. What about you?"

She withdrew into her own space, chewed her lip. "Briefly. Had to, uh, give him away before a move."

She was hiding something. When he pulled in Jenna's driveway, he parked beside Jenna's car. Cut off the engine and faced Lilly. "Tell me what happened."

"It's late. We've had a big day."

"Yes and yes. But I'd like to know about your dog."

She sighed, turned to look him in the eye. Light from the porch and the streetlight illuminated the glint of determination in her eyes. As if it would take strength to get through her story.

"I was engaged once."

He masked his surprise. "Oh?"

"We got a dog together. It lived at his house. Then my fiancé took a job in California." Her tone was direct. Clinical.

Somehow, he hurt worse for her than if she'd been crying. "Is that when you had to give it away?"

"Yes. We'd planned to move right after the wedding."

*Wedding.* It hit him then. Something had gone wrong. He glanced at her hands clutched tightly in her lap before he could stop himself. No ring, of course. Had there ever been a wedding? "What happened?"

She looked away, out the front window, her chin raised high. She took in a shuddering breath. "I found out he cheated on me. The reason he wanted to move across the country was to try to hide his indiscretions."

Indiscretions, plural? Daniel sat rooted to the spot, unable to react. She'd been in love enough to agree to marry, but the jerk had cheated on her.

No wonder she acted scared to death to trust another man.

"I'm sorry," he said, unable to think of anything remotely eloquent or helpful.

She smiled at him, the attempt so pitiful it broke his heart. "It's okay. I'm mostly over it now, thankful I found out in time to break off the engagement."

"But you never got your dog?"

"Clint had sold her to someone in his family and refused to get her back." She huffed out a pent-up breath as if relieved to have finished the conversation. She slung open her door. "Better go check on Quincy."

What kind of scum would do that to a woman he supposedly loved? He walked Lilly to the door and set down the dog supplies, biting his tongue to keep from sharing disparaging comments. She had loved the man, after all.

"You were amazing today with Ricky," he said instead.

She waved off the compliment. "I just talked to him. Nothing special. And for some crazy reason, he likes me."

*Like I do.* He took a step closer, drawn to her generosity, her strength. "I can see why he would."

She took a step away, distrust in her eyes. "He's the wounded drawn to the wounded."

She was so much more than that. He had to let her know he cared. "You may have been wounded in your past, but you're a fighter. Good and trustworthy."

She took another step back for good measure, most likely wishing the sales counter stood between them. "You don't really know me, though. I could have you totally fooled."

A smile pulled at his lips. "I'm a good judge of character."

She stared into his eyes as if trying to determine whether he was telling the truth. As if hoping desperately he was. Hadn't she ever had anyone tell her how wonderful she was?

Unable to fight the temptation any longer, he reached out and touched her cheek. When she didn't draw away but, instead, leaned into his caress, his heart soared. The desire to hold her and protect her raged through him, a powerful drive he couldn't resist.

He pulled her into his arms. "I wish I could take away your painful past," he whispered as he brushed his cheek against her softness, breathing in her sweet scent. "But look at you. You've grown into a caring, strong woman. Fighting for your aunt's store, supporting your sister, helping Ricky."

She whimpered, slid out of his arms. "I should go inside. This—" she gestured to the tiny space between them "—it's not right."

"Felt pretty right to me." He jammed his hands in his pockets, torn in two. How could something so perfect one minute seem wrong the next?

"We're two very different people." Her words, the way she looked at him… She was trying to convince herself as well as him. "I need a man who'll be loyal, dependable, offering security and stability."

Stability. Something he couldn't provide.

She placed her hand in the center of his chest. "You need a woman who's gracious, flexible, willing to serve God with you no matter where you go." Her eyes sought his. "Someone who shares your faith."

She was right, of course. He knew it in sane moments—moments when he wasn't within touching distance of Lilly, moments when she hadn't just shared a piece of herself with him. How could they ever form a real relationship if she didn't first love God?

He forced himself to step away from her touch, turned and headed down the porch steps. Once he had the separation he needed, he looked up. Her eyes shined with moisture. "I care about you, Lilly. But what you've said is true."

She nodded, apparently relieved.

Then a tear slipped down her cheek.

*Lord, help me do what's right.* Only with God's strength did he remain firmly planted on the sidewalk. "Good night, Lilly. Thanks for your help today."

She rapidly blinked, then somehow managed to smile. "I think we made a pretty good team."

He swallowed past the knot in his throat. "Yeah, we did."

Lilly'd had enough. All day she'd tried to be patient with Jenna. But now she had to get her sister out of there. "What's wrong with you?" she whispered after pulling aside Jenna.

"Later," she snarled between clenched teeth.

Lilly sagged into her chair when she realized class time was nearly over. Jenna hadn't alienated anyone yet. *Except me.* Five more minutes…

Ann and the two ladies in the knitting class packed up their supplies and headed toward the door. They had to have noticed Jenna's ongoing snarky comments but had politely ignored them.

Lilly followed them outside to see them off.

On the sidewalk, Vera stopped in her tracks. "Who are those hoodlums over there raking gravel in the parking lot?"

"Hoodlums?" Lilly stepped to where she could view the side parking lot.

"I'd feel a lot safer coming here if you didn't accept help from some work release program," she said, causing concern to draw Flo's normally happy features into a frown.

Lilly spotted Ricky. He had his coat off and wore a T-shirt that revealed muscled arms covered with tattoos. She laughed. "Oh, that's just the high school boys who are doing work for the church."

Vera tsked and headed to her car, Flo following on her heels, checking out the teen guys. Ian and Ricky did look rather scruffy and tough. But not too threatening, surely. Pushing the thought away, Lilly went inside, ready to have it out with her sister. "Why've you been in such a bad mood today?"

Her eyes flashed. "I saw you and Daniel wrapped around each other on the porch last night."

Her heart did a flip-flop. She'd seen?

The memory of Daniel's embrace, of his affirming words, warmed her to her core. She'd experienced something new last night. A man who truly cared. About her. Though the moment had been fleeting, Daniel had helped heal something inside of her.

Lilly chose to be grateful for that moment rather than devastated by the fact that's all it could be—a moment.

"That hug wasn't what it looked like. He was being nice, encouraging me."

With Will on her hip, Jenna took hold of Lilly's upper arm as if she wanted to shake some sense into her. "I see where this is leading. You're going to get hurt."

"Nothing could be further from the truth." Because to get hurt, you had to be in a relationship. And there could be no relationship between the two of them. Period.

Sensing the tension, Will wrapped his arms around his mom's neck.

"Come on, baby. Let's let Aunt Lilly go deal with the supposed hoodlums."

There wouldn't be any dealing with them. They were helping the church. She walked outside and around the side of the building to where Parker, Ian and Ricky spread a load of new gravel the church had bought to extend the parking area.

"Hey!" Parker called. "It's looking good, isn't it?"

"Sure is. Thanks for your hard work."

Ian acknowledged her presence with a quick nod.

Ricky gave an awkward wave. "Hey, Lilly, guess what? Aunt Marla is letting me keep Quincy. I'll pick him up tonight, and he'll stay in the garage until we put in a fence and doghouse."

Apparently, Ricky had moved in, as well. "Great news." Trying to gauge his mood, she approached. "How'd it go last night?"

"Better than I expected." He wiped a shoulder across his forehead and leaned against the rake. "Phil, Marla and I are meeting with Cricket's parents tonight. They're not going to tell her yet."

"Understandable."

He glanced away, and then his gaze finally returned to her eyes. "You know, they may decide not to let me see her."

Given the girl's recent state of mind, that was a possibility. But somehow, she had the sense that they'd allow it. "I doubt they'd do that. They want their daughter to be happy. And their grandchild to have a father in his life."

He shrugged as if he was trying not to get up his hopes. "Daniel said he'd be praying for the meeting. Will you, too?"

Of course, Ricky would assume she was a praying person. She'd attended the church services two weeks in a row.

Her face must've registered surprise or some other emotion, because he immediately began raking again as if to cover embarrassment. "Or not. Maybe it's not your thing."

What could she say? *No, sorry?* "Honestly, I'm not one to pray much."

"No biggie."

"It's just that…well, I fell away from my faith when I was a kid. Guess you can relate, huh?"

"You know it." He shrugged. "It's okay. I don't usually pray, either. Daniel just got me thinking… you know, that God could help me and Cricket."

Her throat tightened. She wanted to reassure him. She even wanted to try to talk to God.

She just didn't know if He'd want to talk to her.

"I hope it goes well tonight," she said, the best she could do at the moment.

"Thanks." Worry dragged down the corners of his mouth as soon as he looked away. He scraped the rake over the rocks.

She really should do this one small thing for Ricky. The thought of praying made her heart begin to pound in her chest. She felt as if she was right at the edge of a precipice about to tumble over. "Hey," she blurted.

Ricky glanced up.

"I'll try to pray for you." The words felt foreign,

as if she'd spoken them in a strange language, her mouth having forgotten how to form the sounds.

But the sky didn't fall. And Ricky didn't laugh at her. In fact, he looked relieved.

"Thanks, Lilly. I'll pray for you, too." He gave a timid grin and then scooted back to work.

His promise of prayer nearly brought her to her knees. It shamed her, as well. If this boy could attempt it, so could she.

Out of the corner of her eye, she spotted Daniel, standing outside the basement door. The expression on his face matched what she'd felt since last night—drained, resigned. He waved.

She longed to go over, chat, spend time together. Instead, she simply waved back. Disappointment churned in her stomach, yet she realized she felt hope also. The hope sparked by a troubled kid who'd said he would pray for her.

As she climbed up the steps of the shop, a car crunched into the lot and gave a short honk of greeting.

Belinda climbed out and hollered, "Hi, Lilly! I'm here to see how you've been doing on your knitting!"

Lilly welcomed her inside. Was there was such a thing as divine timing? Because Belinda had shown up right when Lilly needed her.

She and her friend settled in the gathering area. At Belinda's request, Lilly pulled out her knitting to show what she'd accomplished.

"Wow, you're moving right along!"

"Yeah," she said on a sigh, trying to get worked up about knitting when a billion questions zipped through her mind.

"Lilly, honey, is everything okay?"

The perfect opening. Yet Lilly didn't know how to ask. "Yeah…"

"Daniel told me what happened with the sign company. I'm sorry."

"Live and learn."

Belinda offered a business card to Lilly. "My husband, Geoff, designed and maintains the church's website. It's a hobby, but he's good. He said to tell you, if you're interested, he'd be glad to do yours for free, as well."

Lilly looked into Belinda's kind eyes and thought she might cry. She cleared her throat. "I don't know what to say."

"Check out the church website and see if you like it. Then contact him, if you want. I'm a little partial, of course, but I think he does a marvelous job."

How had she been lucky enough to meet such kind people? "Thank you. I will." Lilly figured the time was now or never. "I need your advice."

Grabbing Lilly's hand, she gave it a squeeze. "Of course."

"One of the boys working with Daniel asked me to pray for him today, and I…well…"

"What is it?"

"I don't feel qualified. I haven't prayed since I was young." There. She'd admitted it. Now her nice, new Christian friend would think she was awful and might not come back.

"I don't think any of us ever feel qualified to talk to the Almighty. But thankfully, we don't have to be. We just have to open up to God, talk to Him, share our hurts and desires. Confess our failings." Belinda patted Lilly's hand. "Anyone can do that, even if it's been years. God loves you and is always seeking to draw you to Him."

She made it sound so easy. "Thanks, Belinda. I feel better now."

She looked at her watch. "Any more questions, you holler, okay? I need to head downstairs for a meeting with Daniel to update him on a ministry I agreed to coordinate."

"Sure. Go ahead."

Her friend started to leave but stopped. Stared at Lilly as if making a decision. "It's a support group for teen girls."

Lilly's heart lurched. "Uh, yeah, he's mentioned it before."

"I know you can't host the group here. But I'd like to invite you to come to a spur-of-the-moment, informal dinner at my house, a kickoff for the new group."

Could Lilly possibly have anything to offer to those girls? Daniel seemed to think so. "I don't know...."

"You'd be great with them. Marla Hartley called

today, told me what happened with Ricky, how you helped. Seems you're a natural with hurting teenagers."

She almost said yes but held back. "I'll think about it."

"Fair enough. Dinner is this Saturday at six-thirty. We'll be meeting regularly on Wednesdays after school." She gave Lilly her address, then pulled her into a quick hug and hopped up. "Hope to see you Saturday...and again Sunday!"

She had no idea what to do about the dinner. Still had a couple days to consider it. At the moment, though, she needed to get back to work.

As Belinda headed downstairs to the basement, Lilly opened the laptop to look up the church's website. If the site looked good, she would call Belinda's husband immediately.

As she was typing in the web address, she noticed she had a new email in her inbox.

From Daniel.

He'd sent the link to a sign company website. Said he'd checked with his former employer—and several recent references—on this one. The company was reliable. When the owner, a college buddy of Daniel's, found out Lilly had been cheated, he offered to do the signs for her at no charge other than the cost of materials.

She reread the message. Yes, he'd really offered to do it for the cost of materials.

And Belinda's husband had generously offered to help, as well.

*God, are You still there, watching out for me after all this time?*

She closed her eyes, and her chest constricted. Mashing a hand against the pressure, she let go of the tears. They made warm paths along her cheeks and dripped off her chin, taking with them some of the pain she'd held in for so long.

Pain of parents who didn't care, of leaving behind people she was fond of each time they'd moved. Pain of believing God must not love her and Jenna, after all, that maybe she'd done something that made her not deserve love.

People in Corinthia had shown so much kindness, she had to consider that maybe God cared about her, too.

*Lord, I'm sorry for how I've acted. I never quit believing, but I ignored You. Blaming You for all the bad stuff in my life, when maybe You've been there all along, waiting for me to turn back to You.*

*Most of all, Lord, please be with Ricky. He and Cricket need You right now.*

She wiped the tears off her face. "And so do I," she whispered. "So do I."

## Chapter Eight

Daniel grabbed his cell phone out of his pocket when a reminder alarm went off. "Time to head over to Belinda's for that dinner I told you about."

"The one with the girls' support group?" Gran asked.

Another much-needed project accomplished, thanks to Belinda. "Yep. I shouldn't be late."

"Oh, wait." She set aside her knitting, pulled off her reading glasses and let them hang around her neck. "I have a message for you here somewhere." She got up and shuffled some magazines on the coffee table. "Here it is. That man from Valdosta called. Asked if you're any closer to determining when you'll move down there."

"Hiding the note from me?" He laughed when she wiggled her brows at him.

She jabbed a finger into his chest. "You know I don't want you to leave. Your church and community love you. Plus, you need to stick around to take care of me in my old age—which, by the way, isn't going to be for a while."

"You're hardy and independent. And besides, if I'm so lovable, the next church should love me, too." He winked, and she teasingly pushed him away.

She plopped back into her chair, her blue eyes losing their humor. "I'm serious, son. It's like you've got ants in your pants. You need to put down roots, fall in love, start a family."

Lilly's face flashed through his brain like a painful lightning strike. Once he got over the shock, he reached for his jacket. "All in good time, GranAnn. God's time."

"Don't let fear stop you."

Fear? He kissed her cheek and then headed for the door. "I'm not afraid. Just doing what I feel called to do."

As he drove to Belinda's, he pondered Gran's words. Why would she think he was afraid to love? He'd simply been too busy to make the effort. Had dated, a couple times seriously. Hadn't found that perfect woman who understood him fully, who understood his calling.

He'd begun to doubt he ever would. Until he met Lilly. In some ways he felt she did understand him.

She knew him well, all right. Well enough to know they weren't right together.

The painful irony left him seriously bummed, yet determined to plow ahead with his plans.

When he went to make a call to Valdosta, he found he had a voice mail.

"Daniel, this is Greg. Just wanted to see if you have an approximate start date. We have a group of fifteen who've committed to join you at the mission church. They're excited and can't wait to meet you."

Daniel was thrilled to have a core group ready to work. *Like Frank and Belinda and the others here.*

It would be difficult to leave, but he'd find a new group of friends and fellow church members.

Daniel called Greg and left a message. Told him he had one more big project—the food pantry in Appleton—to kick off in the next few weeks. If all was well with the church, his best guess was he'd be ready to move in early to mid-summer.

He drew in a tight breath and tried to shake an off-kilter feeling. Come summer, he'd be gone.

He arrived at Belinda and Geoff's house, a large, stone two-story in a swanky neighborhood, and rang the bell.

"Welcome, Daniel!" Belinda brought him into a grand entry and took his coat. "Geoff's not here tonight. He escaped." She laughed as she led Daniel toward the sound of chattering girls.

"I'm not a bit surprised." Geoff wasn't one to hang out with teens. Or people for that matter. He preferred computers and being behind the scenes.

"Girls, this is our pastor, Daniel Foreman."

Cricket and the three girls waved or said hello.

"Hey, ladies. Glad you're joining the group."

"Daniel, we'll introduce everyone once they're all—"

The doorbell chimed. "Oh, there's the last one now."

He headed over and sat beside Cricket, who perched on the end of the couch by herself. She looked much better, yet she still wasn't her old self.

"Hi, Cricket. How are you feeling?"

"Pretty good." She shrugged. "Better, anyway."

He couldn't ask about Ricky. Didn't know if Cricket even knew the boy was pursuing a role in her life.

"Okay, everyone," Belinda called, trying to quiet the room.

He glanced up. Sucked in his breath. *Lilly.* She looked so beautiful in a slim-fitting skirt and boots, paired with a dark green sweater that brought out the green in her eyes.

Eyes that met his and held. She looked radiant… happy. For some strange reason, he had the feeling she was glad to see him.

"Have a seat, everyone. Let's all share our names and maybe tell why you're here, if you feel comfortable."

He glanced at Lilly, who squeezed her hands together as if nervous. She came to take the only seat left—beside him.

Her sweet fragrance teased him. He greeted her then looked away, back to their hostess.

"I'll go first," Belinda said "I'm Belinda, and I'll be facilitating the group—which is a fancy term meaning I'll keep the conversation going, making sure everyone feels included."

A brown-eyed, brown-haired girl who was probably much younger than her provocative clothes suggested waved. "I'm Theresa. I'm here because…well, I don't get along with my parents. They hate my friends. They hate my boyfriend."

"Because he's a creeper," Cricket said, a tiny smile pulling at her lips.

Theresa rolled her eyes. "I'm also here because Cricket invited me. Oh, and I go to the church downtown."

When one of the other girls snorted, Theresa added, "Well, sort of. It's been a while."

"My name's Evette," said the one with bright red, asymmetrically cut hair that was all angles and edges. She flopped back in her chair with a huge sigh. "I'm just here because my mom heard about it and is making me come to keep my driving privileges. Bribery, pure and simple."

"Zaria, here." The girl waved perfectly manicured fingernails, obviously done at a salon. She was modestly dressed in nice clothes. "Similar situation for me. I'm grounded, but my mom knows Belinda." She grinned, her dark, golden-brown eyes sparkling. "Hey, it gets me out of the house. And I'll do anything to keep my car and stay in her good graces."

"And I'm Cricket," she said, smoothing her hands

over her abdomen. "Pretty obvious why I'm here." Her eyes flashed to Daniel. Maybe asking that he not mention the overdose?

He was up next. "As y'all heard, I'm Daniel. I won't be meeting with you weekly. I'm just here to see if you have any questions. To let you know I'm available if you ever need to talk."

"Cool," Evette said.

The girls looked at Lilly, waiting. Probably curious who this other adult was.

"I'm Lilly. I'm fairly new to town. Own the yarn shop above the church with my sister. And I'm here because Belinda's my friend and invited me. And because she thought maybe I could be of some help to you."

Something passed between Lilly and Belinda, and the older woman looked like a proud mother.

"How could you help?" Theresa asked.

Daniel watched Lilly's profile. She swallowed, and her obvious nervousness made him hurt for her.

"Because I went through some tough times when I was a kid."

"You got pregnant?" Cricket asked.

She glanced at Daniel as she turned toward Cricket. "No. But I had trouble with my parents. My dad got fired from a bunch of jobs, so we moved around a lot. I know all about being the new kid, not fitting in."

"My dad lost his job over a year ago," Theresa said. "It's been really hard."

"If you ever want to talk, ask Belinda for my phone number. Or drop by The Yarn Barn."

Belinda stood and clapped her hands together in front of her chest, excited to have everyone in her home. "Okay, ladies…and Daniel. Let's eat! It's in the kitchen. But first, let's bless the food."

Belinda asked Daniel to say a prayer, and they filed into the kitchen. He and Lilly brought up the rear of the line.

"That was brave of you to come, to make yourself available to the girls," he said.

"You encouraged me, and Belinda may have twisted my arm a little." Her eyes lit, again reminding him of how happy she looked. Had something happened—maybe a good day for sales? Ned moving home?

He filled his plate and joined everyone in the dining room. The girls shared stories about the best and worst teachers at school. About the angst of boyfriends…and best friends. About their favorite movies and music.

When Belinda invited the girls to stay a little longer to watch a movie, he and Lilly thanked Belinda and said their good-nights.

He walked Lilly to her car. "Will I see you at services tomorrow?"

"Yes. I— Can you drop by Jenna's for a minute? I'd like to talk to you, show you something."

He wanted to run his fingers through her glorious

curls. If she had any idea of his thoughts, she'd know better than to invite him. "I'll be right behind you."

He followed in his car and met her on the front porch.

"Come in." She showed him into the living room and turned on the lamp. "I'll be right back."

He heard voices in a back room, then she reappeared with a laptop computer.

She closed a set of French doors. "Will's asleep." Then she sat on the couch and patted beside her. "Join me?"

In a heartbeat. *Lord, help me be strong, do the right thing.*

Once he settled on the couch, she turned and faced him. "I've really wanted to tell you something. I wasn't sure I should until tonight."

"What is it, Lilly?"

"Since I've offered to help the girls, I figured you need to know that…well…I've started praying again."

Her words arrowed to his heart, and he froze. "Really?"

True joy radiated from within, making her more beautiful than ever. Probably the change he'd noticed tonight. "Yes."

A simple one-word answer that left him in awe of God's goodness. Afraid to ruin the moment by speaking, he simply smiled. His smile turned into a big grin. Then as her joy washed over him, it turned into a laugh. "I'm glad."

She ran her finger slowly over the computer, tracing an invisible path as if focused on her thoughts. "It started when Ricky asked me to pray for him. Then I talked with Belinda. And now…well, I feel hope for the first time in a long time. I feel like God really does care about me." She burst into action as if unable to hold still another instant, opening her laptop, clicking the keys and spinning it around to face him. "Look."

A basic website template with The Yarn Barn at the top of the page showed on her screen.

"Did you do that?" he asked.

"No. Geoff Hodges offered to do it. The site's in the beginning stages, something he threw together quickly. But he's doing it at no charge. Out of the goodness of his heart." Her eyes nearly glowed, and awe shone on her face.

He choked a giant boulder from his throat. Belinda's husband had done the church website as a gift to the church. Daniel appreciated it, but looking at Lilly, he could see what a gift like that would mean for someone who apparently didn't have people doing kind acts for her very often. "That's great."

"He's even going to take some photos I shot of the yarns and the building and do a logo for us to put in the banner at the top of each page." She snapped the laptop closed. "I wanted to let you know what's going on, in case you worried about me working with the girls without…you know…having God in my life. Because I do."

He suddenly felt like he couldn't get a deep enough breath. *Lord, does this change things?* He stood and shoved his hands into his pockets. "That's great Lilly. Of course, I trust you with the teenagers."

He had to get out of there. To determine how her newly rekindled faith changed their situation—if at all.

She followed him to the door and stilled, staring at his chest as if she couldn't quite look him in the eye. She ran her finger over his sleeve like she had been running it over the laptop, as if she didn't even realize she was doing it. "I have so much to be thankful for."

He held his breath, afraid to move, afraid to speak. He wanted to lift her chin, to get her to look at him. But he didn't dare touch her. "The Hodges are generous people."

"You are, too."

His mouth went dry. When she looked up, gratitude and affection in her eyes, he felt as if someone grabbed hold of his heart and yanked. "I don't understand," he said through vocal cords that felt like sawdust.

"The signs for the shop. I talked to your friend. He's going to get started this week and work on them as he has time."

In all his life, he'd never wanted so badly to touch someone, to hold her, take care of her. "It was the least I could do after the previous mess up."

"No, it's more than that. Belinda and her husband, your sign-maker friend…you. You're all kind and generous, and I think the reason is because you love God and try to do what's right."

Her hand, still on his arm, warmed him through the fabric of his shirt. She blinked her big hazel eyes, the long dark lashes casting a brief shadow on her cheeks. Then those lashes swept upward and her heart shone in her eyes.

His gaze dropped to her full lips, lips he'd dreamed about. She was sweet and giving and was looking at him as if she wanted this, too. So he lowered his head, ever so slowly and—

The French doors burst open like the shot of a cannon in the quiet room. Jenna stood staring at them.

As he took a step away from Lilly, her hand fell from his arm.

"What are your intentions with my sister?" Jenna asked, a tremble in her voice.

Lilly stepped forward, almost as if getting between him and her sister, a protective gesture that touched him.

He stepped beside Lilly. "I—"

"No," Lilly said, grabbing hold of his arm. "You're not going to answer that."

Jenna stood apart from them, as if drawing a line in the sand, declaring battle. "I won't watch you hurt my sister."

"There's no hurting going on, here," Lilly said. "I

was telling him about how I've turned back to God, how I'm praying again for the first time in years." Tears filled her eyes. "Please don't embarrass me by accusing him of doing something wrong when we were just sharing a...a close moment."

Jenna frantically blinked at tears. "He's a church starter, Lilly. I heard he's already got the next church waiting for him in South Georgia."

"Your sister knows all that," Daniel said. "And she's shared how important stability is for her. We understand we're living two different lives."

The words sank like lead in his stomach. Tonight, briefly, he'd thought maybe they had a chance. But Jenna reminded him of the other issues still keeping them apart.

"Don't do anything you'll regret," Jenna said to her sister. "Because men will walk out on you faster than you can say *Jack Robinson.*"

"I'm an adult and will make my own decisions."

Jenna's shoulders slumped. "You two can deny it all you want, but you have feelings for each other. You need to deal with them."

Will's cry sounded over the baby monitor. Jenna reached for the doors. "If you ask me, the best way would be to stay away from each other till Daniel's gone." She quietly closed the doors behind her.

Lilly opened her mouth to speak, then stopped.

"Your sister is just worried about you. And she's right, you know."

"Her outlook is colored by Ned's leaving."

"She's right about our feelings."

Her eyes fell closed. She huffed out a breath. "I don't want to get hurt again."

They were in an impossible situation. "I don't want to hurt you."

"Then I guess we follow her advice."

Why had he admitted his feelings? Surely ignoring them would be easier than staying away from Lilly. "I'll do my best."

He headed out the door but turned back as she was shutting it behind him. "I want you to feel free to come to church services and take part in ministries. We can handle that."

She nodded. "Yeah, okay." She gazed into his eyes for one brief moment. Then she shut the door.

He closed himself in his car with his misery and regret.

Tonight, they'd kicked off a program for troubled teen girls. He'd gotten one step closer to reaching his goals for the church. But he'd lost so much more.

Lilly hurt for a week, her stomach in a tight knot, struggling to make it through everyday activities. She avoided Daniel and struggled in her prayer life. But on the following Sunday morning, she woke with the sun and made a decision.

*No more.*

God loved her and had a plan for her. And even if that plan didn't include Daniel, she had a reason to move on. She wanted to make a success of her new business. And even more, to work on her growing relationship with God.

Over the next few weeks, as the cold weather warmed and daffodils pushed up through the ground, she did just that. Her friendship with Belinda grew as The Yarn Barn's business grew. Thanks to the Hodgeses, their customer base increased significantly. They'd even set up online ordering, and internet orders had exploded. She'd paid their suppliers, the utility bills and had a good chunk of the next quarterly tax payment.

She'd even picked up her camera again and had been snapping shots of the support group girls whenever she hung out with them. She had an idea for an article and called a friend in Louisville who owned a magazine. The woman had been hounding Lilly for years to come work with her. They planned to meet sometime in July.

Lilly closed her laptop, the hustle and bustle of people gathering for the church service downstairs pulling her away from checking new online orders. The bells on the front door drew her attention.

Jenna breezed in with a smile as she lifted Will higher up on her hip. "Sorry I'm late. I thought Will was trying to take his first step, but it turned out he had his hand on the table."

"What a big boy!" Lilly said to Will as she clapped her hands and reached out for him. "You'll be off and running before we know it."

"I guess we need to head downstairs." Jenna sighed, as if the effort were odious.

She and Jenna had gotten along better since she had been avoiding contact with Daniel. Jenna seemed relieved, though she still refused counseling and hadn't patched up her relationship with Ned. But she'd at least tried attending the services the past couple Sundays, hoping to find common ground with her husband.

"I'm ready." Lilly had attended every service since she'd started praying again and had asked God back into her life. She'd sat in the back during worship with Belinda and Geoff, plus Jenna when she came. Then Lilly would slip out as quickly as possible afterward, before Daniel made it to the door. If he got to the door first, she would exit by way of the inside stairs.

The system of avoidance had worked well. Or maybe the success was simply because Daniel was practicing avoidance, as well. Whatever the reason, Lilly hadn't talked to Daniel other than a polite hello for almost a month.

Jenna handed Will to the nursery worker in the back corner, and this time he went without a hitch. "I can't believe I keep doing this for my husband."

"You need to be doing it for you." She gave her sister a knowing stare, waiting for the anticipated reaction.

But this time, Jenna didn't explode into her usual

rant. "You've changed, you know," she said as she seriously studied Lilly. "Inside and out."

"I guess prayer does that. God does that."

"So you're really feeling this?"

"I am." She smiled at her sister as they headed for their "regular" chairs. "You were probably too young to remember when that church bus would pick us up for Sunday school when we were little, but I do. The people were so good to us. I feel that here, too."

Jenna wrinkled her nose as if she didn't agree.

"At the first service we attended over at Frank's, when you ran out crying, I thought maybe you were feeling a pull back to the church, too," Lilly whispered.

"No, I was just torn up about Ned leaving." Something in Jenna's eyes said otherwise, though. She looked away, as if she wasn't telling Lilly the whole truth.

Lilly didn't push. God would work on Jenna in His own good time.

"So do you think you might stay on after the year is up?" Jenna asked as nonchalantly as she might ask what Lilly wanted for dinner. "Because I can see us doing the shop together for a long time, especially if we can make a decent income."

Unease crept into the calm Lilly had worked hard to maintain. "You know I've always dreamed of using my degree. I figure my half of the money from the shop will help me build my freelance business. I've already set up a July meeting with my friend, who has the magazine in Kentucky. Have been working on a piece about troubled teens."

Jenna sighed and waved at the Hodgeses, who'd walked in. "You sacrificed to put me through college. It's only fair you get your chance for a change. It's just…well, I've gotten used to having you around."

Music started, a soft praise song on the keyboard, as they began the service. Daniel's voice flowed over Lilly like a comforting cloak, but the sound also reminded her of the pain of their last night together. She tried her best to push the thoughts from her mind and to focus.

But she could barely sit still throughout the worship service. Jenna's words had made her antsy. She caught herself considering staying in Corinthia with these people. While they sang, Lilly glanced around at once-unfamiliar faces that belonged, now, to friends.

Frank gave a friendly wink as they finished the last song. He'd fed her and Jenna lunch at the same table in his restaurant the past two weeks. Might he someday ask if she wanted her regular?

She glanced up as Daniel invited them to bow their heads for the closing prayer. Seeing him always took her breath away, made her wish her situation were different.

When the prayer was over, she went into her quick-escape maneuver. She beat Daniel outside and let out her pent-up breath. The slight embarrassment at being so juvenile didn't diminish her sense of relief one bit.

"Hey, Lilly, wait up," someone called.

She turned and found Ricky and Cricket holding hands. Ricky had been faithfully coming to church each week, every time the door was open. Just like Lilly had. It seemed the two of them had followed a similar path in their faith journeys.

"Hi, you two."

Ricky and Cricket's families had worked together and were allowing Ricky and Cricket to see each other, allowing Ricky to be supportive. But this was the first time Cricket had come out in public with him.

Ricky swung their joined hands to his lips and kissed her knuckles. "Her parents are allowing us to officially date now."

"Yep." She laughed, her silky blond hair swinging. "No more chaperones."

The young couple looked adoringly at each other. The tenderness and affection between them gripped her heart, made her ache for the same.

No one would be looking at Lilly that way anytime soon.

Cricket looked so young, Lilly couldn't believe she'd be having a baby in a couple months. A scarier time than usual for a teenaged mom since they'd worry about the possible effects of the overdose.

"So, Cricket, how are the meetings with Belinda going?" Lilly asked.

"Belinda's great. She's really helping me deal with…well, everything."

"Yeah, she's the best." Someone else Lilly would have to leave behind once she moved away.

"Quincy misses you. You should come visit him sometime," Ricky said.

Tears prickled behind her nose. "I'd love that. I'll come by soon."

Why was everything hitting her so hard today? She needed to get a grip on her emotions.

But she couldn't. She fought tears all the way around the building as she headed to her car.

Everything had been going so well these past few weeks—everything that didn't have to do with Daniel. But she'd been careless, apparently. Had allowed herself to settle in. To love the community they'd built at the yarn shop. Love her new friends. Love her church.

Not to mention growing closer than ever to Ann, Belinda, Jenna and Will.

In just a few months, she'd move away and would only visit for holidays. How would she ever leave them?

A horn honked out front. Lilly turned and saw Ann getting out of an expensive black sedan.

"Hello, Lilly!" She waved as she approached in her baby blue pantsuit and pearls that she'd most likely worn to church. She limped along slowly, a cane in one hand. Lilly couldn't remember ever seeing the cane before. Alarm shot through her. What if something happened to Ann? She'd helped fill the hole Talitha's death had left in their lives.

"Hi, Ann. Are you okay?"

"Can't complain. But I'd be better if you and your sister and nephew would come for lunch today. I won't take no for an answer."

"Oh, Ann, I'm sorry, but we can't. Jenna has a meal planned."

"I said I won't take no for an answer. Talitha asked me to watch out for you girls, and I feel like I've fallen down on my duty. You must come so I don't feel guilty." She smiled, her blue eyes hopeful. Bright red lipstick feathered into creases from years of smiling. Her excited expression made it impossible to refuse.

Lilly glanced at the car, wondering if they were picking up Daniel, hoping he wouldn't be at lunch.

"That's my son-in-law, Blake, driving me. He'll be joining us."

She hadn't mentioned Daniel. Maybe he had a meeting or something to do. Her tension unfurled, leaving her relieved…and disappointed.

Disappointed? *Shame on you, Lilly Barnes.*

"I'll have to talk to Jenna. But even if she can't come, I will. You're so nice to invite us."

"It's my pleasure. Y'all come over to the house as soon as you can."

Ann hurried back to Blake's car, moving faster

this time. Without using the cane. Maybe the prospect of having some company lifted her spirits.

Lilly headed home to try to convince Jenna to come along to lunch. It took fifteen minutes of cajoling, but she finally agreed. They showed up at Ann's half an hour after the invitation.

When the door swung open, Lilly couldn't believe her luck.

Determined to make it through one day without doing something to antagonize Jenna or his dad, Daniel had prepared to paste a friendly expression on his face when he answered the door. But as he pushed open the screen door and came within touching distance of Lilly for the first time in weeks, he found he didn't have to exert any effort at all. One look into her eyes, and his smile formed of its own volition.

"Hi," he said, close enough that he could smell her sweet, flowery fragrance.

Her teeth worried with her lower lip. He tried really hard not to look in the direction of her lips, but with no success. His heart raced as he tried to drag his gaze upward. Could she tell her nearness tortured him?

The corners of her mouth formed into the tiniest of smiles. "Hi."

Jenna cleared her throat. "Don't mind me. I'll just head back to the kitchen."

He nodded toward her retreating figure "Wow. She left you alone with me?"

Lilly's laugh poured over him like warm syrup. "She's talked to Ned some this week. Is in a pretty good mood—comparatively." She held out a plastic container. "Thanks for inviting us. I brought some chocolate cake Jenna baked last night."

"Thanks." He took the cake from her but didn't make a move toward the kitchen. "I—"

"We—" she said at the same time.

They laughed, and some of the tension left the room.

She'd worked so hard to avoid him around the church the past few weeks that he'd feared she was going to give herself whiplash. Of course, he'd pretty much done the same.

"Look, Lilly, I know this is awkward. But I appreciate you coming. For GranAnn's sake."

"She's kind to invite us."

"Are you doing okay?"

Her eyes were clear and bright, like someone who was happy, at peace. "I'm doing great. Physically and spiritually."

He reached out, wanting to hug her, but rubbed her shoulder instead. "I've been glad to see you at church. Hear you've attended a couple of the girls' support group meetings."

"Lilly," Jenna called. "Bring the cake."

Lilly chuckled, shook her head. "Maybe we should…

uh…go on back?" She nodded toward the kitchen area. "You know, before she sends a search party."

When he walked into the kitchen, everyone was seated around the table except for Gran, who stirred something on the stove. Blake was stony-faced as usual. Not hostile. Yet not welcoming.

Daniel gestured to the high chair beside Jenna. "Would you like Will to use this?"

"Yes, thank you."

Her words were polite. Her tone said she still hadn't forgotten that he'd nearly kissed her sister.

He held out his arms for Will. "Ready to go, big guy?"

Will giggled and reached for him.

"*Big guy* is his special name that only his dad calls him," Jenna said, clearly sending Daniel a warning.

Blake's eyes widened, surprised, and then they narrowed. Daniel prayed he wouldn't say anything, that he'd accept Jenna's dislike for his son and let it go.

Daniel went to his regular chair beside Jenna, hoping he could somehow mend the rift between them.

"No, son. Sit over here beside Lilly," Gran said. "We have one more guest coming. He'll be late, said to get started."

"Who's coming, Ann?" Blake asked.

"Ned, Jenna's husband." She patted Jenna and joined them at the table.

All eyes turned toward Jenna. She seemed flustered, but then she recovered, gave a weak smile. "Thank you, Miss Ann."

Once Blake blessed the meal, and platters of food were being passed around, he questioned Lilly and Jenna about their family. Their answers were vague, and the conversation didn't last long.

While Jenna fed Will, Daniel asked Lilly if the new website was finished, how the signs were working out, how business was going. All the questions he'd wanted to ask for the past month.

Lilly lit up as she filled him in on all the improvements. "Everything's going well."

"You two sound like you never see each other," Blake said, confusion drawing his eyebrows downward. "I thought you shared the same building."

Awkward moment.

Daniel busied himself buttering a biscuit. "We're both busy and don't run into each other except for Sundays."

"And then he's always talking to church members," Lilly added. "And I'm hurrying to…uh…leave."

Flee, more like it. He bit back a smile.

Daniel's dad studied the two of them.

"Jenna," Ann said, "is Will walking yet?"

Nice move. Grandmother to the rescue.

"No, he's only eleven months old. But he's sure trying, cruising around everywhere."

A knock sounded on the back door as it squeaked opened. "Anyone here?" Ned called.

"Dada!" Will bounced in the high chair, reaching for his father.

"Come in, come in!" Ann hopped up to introduce him to Blake and show him to his seat—conveniently located next to Jenna.

Before he sat, he reached across Jenna and picked up Will. "Hey, big guy." He didn't put him back in his chair, but sat with Will in his lap and must've kissed his son's head a dozen times.

The affection between them was enough to put a lump in Daniel's throat.

He pulled away his attention from the happy father-son interaction and ended up looking at Lilly, whose face nearly glowed with joy as she watched the scene.

"Ned, we're glad you could make it," Lilly said. "Jenna and I missed you at church."

"Y'all went?" Ned asked his wife.

"Yes." The hope on Jenna's face made Daniel look away, a moment too private to witness.

"Well, I'm sorry I missed it. I filled in for Porter. Now *he's* got the flu."

As they passed the serving dishes to Ned, Jenna spooned baby food into Will's mouth, right there in Ned's lap, a perfect family scene.

Daniel imagined how it might be Sunday after Sunday if you had extended family living nearby. Dinner together after church. Babies passed around, loved and cherished. Generations tied together by the bonds of blood and marriage.

His gaze was drawn again to Lilly, hair pulled back at the top in some kind of clip. He'd missed her terribly. Missed talking with her, teasing her, watching her interact with the kids around the church.

Her skin, smooth and golden, glowed as she smiled over quiet conversation with his grandmother.

Peace washed over him. A peace he didn't often feel unless he was praying. This felt right.

He could get used to this. Sitting around a table and sharing a weekly meal with Lilly. With his family and her family.

But God had called him elsewhere…hadn't He?

Yes, definitely. The move to Valdosta was falling into place. They were expecting him, counting on him.

"I hear y'all had a big fire the other night," Blake said to Ned. "Were you working?"

"Yeah. Sad situation. The family lost their home. But at least they all got out."

Jenna gripped Ned's arm. "I didn't know you were working that night. Were you one of the ones they mentioned on the news who went in to rescue the grandmother?"

Ned's face reddened across his cheeks. "Yeah. But it was Bobby who got hurt the worst. I only had a few stitches."

"Stitches?" Jenna whispered, as if she could hardly utter the words.

He glanced at his plate, obviously uncomfortable with the attention. "Just doin' my job."

"If you would come home, I'd know your work schedule. I'd know when to check on you at the hospital."

Ned nodded toward GranAnn. "Jenna, hon, we can talk about this later after we finish this wonderful meal Ann cooked."

Tears fell down her cheeks, and Daniel knew she wasn't going to drop the subject like her husband had asked.

"Please come home."

Lilly jumped up. "Will, sweetie, how about going outside with Aunt Lilly?" She gave her nephew a reassuring smile and took him out of Ned's lap. She hurried out the back door.

"Jenna," Daniel said, "I'd be happy to talk with you and Ned if you'd like to meet at my office later."

"Not when you and the church are the ones keeping him too busy to come back to his family."

Blake put his hands flat on the table. "My son would do no such thing. You should appreciate his offer." He pushed up from his chair. "Ann, thank you for lunch, but I need to go."

Stunned, Daniel said, "It's okay, Dad."

"Blake, please," Ann said. "Ned and Jenna have had a tough time lately, so they need our support."

Tears streamed down Jenna's face, and she swiped

her hand across a running nose. "What I need is my husband to come home."

"I want to come home. Say the word, promise you'll come to counseling with me, and I'll pack up and move back home today."

Jenna stood up so quickly that the chair scooted backward and hit the kitchen cabinet. She appeared startled that she'd done it. "I'm sorry, everyone." Sucking in a wobbly breath, she looked at her husband. "It's your day with your son. Please bring him home by seven." Then she hurried out.

Ned looked miserable. Embarrassed. "I apologize for airing our dirty laundry at your table when you've been so nice."

"Don't you worry," Ann said. "We'll keep praying for you."

"I'm going to go try to talk to her," he said as he pushed his chair under the table, then carried his dishes to the sink. "Daniel, could you ask Lilly to watch Will this afternoon, and give them a ride home? I'll leave Will's car seat out front."

As soon as Daniel agreed, Ned headed out after his wife.

Blake stood by the back door ready to escape the commotion. "Well, that was a stressful meal. What'd you do to get on that woman's bad side?"

Of course, his dad would assume he was to blame. But, he'd also stuck up for Daniel, a real shocker. "Nothing." Except nearly kiss her sister. "She blames me for Ned's involvement in the church, which she sees as a threat."

"I sure hope they'll come meet with you, Daniel," Gran said.

"They'd be lucky to have his counseling." Blake gave a firm nod.

Had his dad just affirmed his new career? "Thanks."

"Oh, don't look so flabbergasted. I've been watching you. You do good work at that church of yours." His dad looked uncomfortable, as if it pained him to say it.

Gran glowed.

"Well, I guess I'll go fill in Lilly on her job as babysitter for the day."

As he passed by his dad, Blake stopped him. "Do you think your feelings for Lilly are what set off Jenna?"

Daniel's heart thudded in his chest. "My feelings?"

Blake shook his head. "Oh, come on. You can't try to deny it. I see how you look at her. How she looks at you."

That last half of his statement, the part about Lilly looking at him, made the thudding speed up. "What do you mean?"

"Don't act ignorant. You and Lilly have feelings for each other. Is there a reason you're not acting on them?"

*You bet there is.* "I admit I'm attracted to her.

Who wouldn't be? She's beautiful and kind and generous…"

"Amen to that," his grandmother said, inching her way into the conversation. "I thought you'd never notice."

Oh, he'd noticed all right. "But she's leaving once the terms of her aunt's will are fulfilled. And I'm leaving as soon as I've met my goals for the church and God is ready for me to move on."

He hated to crush his grandmother's hope, but he had to be open about the impossibility of a relationship with Lilly. "I'm sorry to disappoint you, GranAnn. But Lilly craves stability after the childhood she had. Marrying someone like me, who'll always be moving around, would be impossible."

"I wasn't talking marriage," Blake said. "Just exploring how you feel about each other." He waved his hand at Daniel. "Never mind. You go ahead and keep trying to fool yourself."

Fooling himself? Could he be?

No. He and Lilly were both being realistic, responsible. They each had a plan and needed to stick with it.

Lilly sat on the picnic table bench facing outward, Will in her lap trying to reach for nearby tulips.

Jenna and Ned had been doing better that week. He'd dropped by, they'd talked, had dinner together. But they'd just proved what Lilly had known all along—that life could go crazy at any time. And that in one minute, any progress you'd made could be wiped out by stubbornness or insecurity.

Lilly didn't want that to happen to her. She didn't want to waste any more time wallowing in her past. God had given her a fresh start. She felt His presence more than ever as she spent time with Him each day.

She glanced up when she heard the back door close. Daniel. Just the person she needed to talk to.

"Hey," he said. "You've got Will for the afternoon. Ned went chasing after Jenna."

She tuned out her sister's marital problems and focused on what had been pounding through her head since she walked out the door.

"God's been working on me. Convicting me," she said.

He didn't look surprised to hear her talking about God. He looked seriously interested. "About what?"

"I want to make a difference. Especially after that debacle in there." She rubbed her hand over Will's sweet, soft head. "I want to help girls who've had unhappy childhoods or have made bad decisions. I want to help them heal before they grow up frightened, pushing people away. Like Jenna…like me." She looked up at him, the sun momentarily blinding her.

He sat down beside her on the wooden bench, his warm body a nice contrast to the cool air. "What would you like to do?"

Now that he was beside her, she could see the blue of his eyes that matched the cloud-laced sky. Could see the tender look. Could see that he was pleased by her decision.

"I want to host the girls' support group at the shop. I want to teach Cricket and her friends to knit."

His teasing grin sent her stomach on a quick, wild ride.

"Or maybe I should simply aim to learn alongside them and let Belinda do the teaching."

He reached out and gently brushed his knuckles across her cheek. "I've been an idiot. My own dad told me so."

She couldn't respond. His touch left her breathless, and a little addled.

"I can't deny my feelings anymore, Lilly."

She sucked in air like a person drowning. "We've talked about this. A relationship is impossible."

"Impossible, yes." He leaned closer, stopping just short of touching his lips to hers. "But undeniable."

When he looked from her lips to her eyes, she was lost. She grasped for a last line of defense, anything to keep her from closing the tiny space between them. "We don't have to act on the feelings, though."

"I do." He wrapped his arm around her waist, scooting her yet closer. He caressed her cheek with his rough, warm hand. Ran his thumb over her bottom lip. "I'm going to kiss you now, no matter who comes out that door or tries to stop me."

A nervous laugh slipped out of her, but the sound was deep and husky, strange to her ears. When he took her face between his hands and touched his lips to hers, the universe expanded behind her closed eyes. Joy blossomed and spread into all the empty places inside her, smoothing over the raw edges of hurt.

Daniel cared about her.

And no matter how much time they would end up having together before they parted ways, her life would be forever changed.

Her nephew suddenly struggled to pull away, trying to get out of her lap. With all the willpower she could muster, she ended the kiss. She wanted to groan in frustration but instead, she stood and set Will on his feet, holding on to his hands. He stomped at the grass.

Her eyes flicked to Daniel standing beside her. His satisfied expression sent a thrill through her. "At least you're not going to apologize and say it shouldn't have happened," she said.

"No way. That kiss has been a long time coming."

Will let go of one hand and took a step. She leaned forward and held on.

Daniel walked beside them. "But it does complicates matters."

"Again, words a woman longs to hear. That she complicates some poor guy's life."

Daniel chuckled as he took Will's other hand. Her nephew took two steps between them and then let go of Lilly. He continued pulling Daniel along.

Daniel looked back over his shoulder. "Complication or not, I needed to tell you how I feel."

Had he needed to kiss her, as well? Heat crept up her neck, betraying her. "So what now?" she asked, wishing that for once she wouldn't actually voice the thoughts in her head.

As Daniel slowed, Will pulled away his hand. He took one step. And a second step on his own. Then on the third attempt, he plunked downward onto his diapered backside, his mouth wide open.

Lilly gasped and clapped her hands. "You did it, Will! You took your first steps!"

Will looked pleased with himself, clapping his own hands.

"Nice job, Will," Daniel said, gazing at Lilly the whole time, warming her with his attention, making her feel special.

"What next?" he repeated. "You saw the kid. You just take off and go, even if you're in new territory and have no idea what you're doing."

She laughed. "We may fall on our rear ends."

Daniel nodded at Will. "He's still grinning."

She wasn't sure she was ready for new territory. But the confidence on Daniel's face made her want to dare to go there. To give it a try. "I guess we'll learn as we go."

He pulled away his gaze and picked up her nephew. "Come on little man, we should probably take you home to your mom so she can see your new trick. We don't want her mad at us."

*Jenna.* Lilly had to go home and face Jenna. To tell her she'd missed her son's first steps. To tell her that Lilly had committed to hosting one of the church ministries.

But she wouldn't tell her that she'd just kissed a man whose calling would eventually lead him away from her.

## Chapter Nine

The following week, Lilly stood shoulder to shoulder with Belinda and admired the class table they'd set up for Cricket, Zaria, Theresa and Evette, who'd be coming to the shop that afternoon for their support group meeting.

Each place had a skein of yarn and pair of brand-new knitting needles. Belinda had been thoughtful enough to make tote bags for everyone, stitching a monogram on each—including one for Lilly.

"I still can't believe you made one for me," she said to her friend.

"You need one, too!"

Yeah, her freebie canvas bag had seen better days. "So what are we going to discuss today?"

"As you've seen from the meetings you've attended, I usually let them chat first. Then I try to draw them out, get them to talk about problems. We discuss solutions and choices. All very laid-back since I'm simply here to love and support them."

Lilly ran a finger over her embroidered initials, remembering how other girls in middle school had written their initials using their boyfriends' last names. She'd never dared. "You're a blessing. I wish I'd had someone like you around when I was a kid."

Lilly's cell phone vibrated in her pocket. As a car crunched on gravel out front, she opened the text message from Jenna.

Fed Will his lunch and put him down for a nap here at home. Won't condone something that'll end up hurting you. See you tonight.

Lilly wanted to shake some sense into her sister, to shake her until her teeth rattled. On Sunday, Jenna had been upset as anticipated. But then she'd overreacted by associating Lilly's support group involvement as involvement with Daniel.

Apparently, she'd decided to boycott the class. Preventing Lilly from focusing on the girls. Forcing her to divide her time between the group and helping customers. "Come on, let's go see if that's the girls who arrived."

She and Belinda stepped outside to the front steps. A warm spring day greeted them, the sun shining high in the sky with not a cloud in sight.

Her heart shot up into her throat when she noticed Daniel and the guys working. She hadn't seen Daniel in two days, not since they'd kissed—and then had the run-in with Jenna.

Daniel, Parker, Ian, Ricky along with Darren, from Ricky's apartment complex, were at the sides of the steps digging with shovels, building plant beds to adorn the front of the shop. When Daniel looked up and smiled, her pulse rate shot into dangerous territory.

"Hi, Darren," she said. "I'm glad you came."

"It's Dag, remember?" the boy said, his face bright red as he looked to the cool older guys to make sure they weren't going to tease him.

"Hey, Ricky," Cricket called from the open door of the vehicle that had just pulled in, drawing everyone's attention away from Dag.

Ricky dropped his shovel as if he forgot it was in his hand and hurried over to help her from the car. He gave her a quick, awkward hug and a kiss on the cheek.

The other doors burst open, and three girls climbed out.

"Come on in, girls," Belinda said as they approached the steps. "We're ready for you."

Ian, who still hadn't attended worship services and had apparently not yet seen Cricket, stared at her extended belly. He swallowed as if a baseball were stuck in his throat. Maybe the shock of seeing the girl pregnant would serve as a word of caution for him.

Lilly hustled the girls inside so the boys could get back to work, and then on to their homework.

As she shut the door, she looked down at Daniel—couldn't resist.

He gave her a thumbs-up.

Feeling silly, she gave him one in return.

"Isn't Jenna here?" he asked.

"No. She decided to put Will down for a nap at home."

He appeared to understand the part she'd left unsaid and gave her an apologetic look. "I hope the meeting goes well."

She didn't know what to say, so she gave him another goofy thumbs-up and hustled inside.

The expressions on the girls' faces as they checked out their personalized tote bags from Belinda were priceless. The gifts made them feel as special as Lilly had.

"Hey, do y'all mind if I take some photos?" Lilly asked.

"Fine with me," Cricket said. The others agreed.

She started snapping shots of them admiring their new bags. "I thought it would be fun to follow your progress on the projects."

"Okay, girls," Belinda said, herding Zaria and Cricket toward their chairs. "I want to show you how to get started knitting. Then once you get the hang of it, we'll talk."

Once she taught them how to cast on and do a simple knit stitch, she looked at Lilly. "Why don't you show them your scarf?"

Sharing her less-than-perfect work might encourage the girls. "I'm still learning and practicing," she said as she held up her half-done scarf that looked as if a kindergartner could have done it.

"You mean you own this place and don't even know how to knit?" asked Zaria.

"It's true."

"Oh, man, that's awesome," Evette said. "Kind of like Theresa being in high school."

Theresa's head jerked up from her knitting. "What's that supposed to mean? I'm dumb?"

"Hey, none of that," Belinda said. "Remember what we talked about last week? Being kind to each other. Trying to understand we all have problems no matter what things look like on the outside."

"Yeah, Miss Goody Two-Shoes has problems, all right. The problem of deciding between carrying Coach or Dooney & Bourke to school each day. Rough life," said Evette.

"That's not funny. Besides, my handbags are old, from before my dad lost his job." Theresa pursed her lips and focused on the yarn, jabbing a needle through the yarn loop and then pulling too quickly. Two stitches fell off. "See what you made me do?"

Zaria gave another of her snorts, obviously siding with Evette in laughing at Theresa.

"Come on, you two, be nice," Cricket said. "I'm stuck. I think I messed up on the last stitch."

As Belinda helped the girl, Lilly worked on her own scarf, wondering what she'd gotten herself into with this group. She hadn't dealt well with girl relationships as a kid. Never really had the chance. How did she think she could possibly have something to offer?

About the time she finished one row of her scarf, the bells jangled, letting her know a customer had arrived.

Thankful business had picked up, she left Belinda and the girls.

She headed to the front. "Oh, hi, Vera. What can I do for you?"

"I'm tired of the shawl I've been working on. I want to start a new project. A nice gift for an old friend."

About the time Vera had narrowed her choice to two different yarns, the front bell rang again. Another new customer.

"Vera, if you don't mind, I'll leave you a minute to make your decision. Just holler when you're ready."

Lilly scurried over to a cute young woman holding a pattern she'd printed off the internet. "I want to make this, but I don't have a clue how to start."

While she helped the woman pick out supplies and gave her a flyer about the knitting class, the front bell rang again.

"I'll be right with you," Lilly called.

When the front bell rang a fourth time, she wanted to cry, then thought better of it. *Lord, though it looks as if I won't get to meet with the girls at all, thank You for these customers.* "Feel free to look around," she called in the general direction of the door. "I'll be right with you."

Heavy footsteps headed her way as she rang up the first purchase. She glanced up as she placed the items in a bag.

Daniel's handsome face stopped her midmotion. "Oh, hi, Daniel."

"Came to see if I can help since Jenna's not here today."

He'd come to her rescue. Because he knew how much it would mean to her to be able to help the girls.

Her heart soared, and the smile she gave the young customer as she handed over the shopping bag felt as if it stretched her mouth to its limits. "Thank you. I hope you'll be able to make the next class."

The pretty woman's gaze darted to Daniel, and she blushed. "I think I will."

Lilly fought the insane urge to say, *Back off. He's mine.*

But one kiss didn't infer ownership. It didn't even, technically, infer a relationship. Though, in her book, it should.

Lilly held her pleasant expression in place. "Good. We'll look forward to seeing you."

As the beautiful customer left, she noticed Daniel didn't pay the woman a bit of attention. He simply stared into Lilly's eyes as if waiting for her to say something. For the first time in ages, she felt beautiful. "Thanks for showing up."

He nodded at Vera and the remaining woman looking through the yarn bins. "I'll do my best to help them. Go back to the group."

She knew he might be clueless about yarn and knitting, but he certainly had a way with the ladies. She had a feeling she'd be leaving her business in good hands. "Thank you. Holler if you have someone paying with a credit card or if you need me."

She hurried back to the circle around the table. As she picked up her scarf and needles, he said, "Ladies, what can I do for you?" in his most charming voice.

One of them tittered. The other, Vera from the sound of her voice, told him maybe he could help her make a decision. Their voices faded as Daniel skillfully moved them away from the gathering area.

"I'm such a spaz," Zaria said. "See how awful this looks." She held up two rows, the beginning of her scarf.

"You know," Theresa said, holding up her nicely progressing scarf, "I think I've done this before. I think Miss Ann showed me and Chelsea Reynolds how to knit a long time ago."

Evette shook her head and made a disgusted face. "Another goody-goody," she mumbled under her breath.

"Who's Chelsea?" Belinda asked as she helped Cricket fix a dropped stitch.

"Chelsea Reynolds. My former best friend from kindergarten up."

"So you're not friends now?" Lilly asked.

Without skipping a beat in her knitting, Theresa let out a huge sigh. "No. Her dad's the police chief, and he won't let her hang out with me anymore."

'You're better off," Evette said. "Who needs the law on your back constantly?"

"I miss her." The words came out quietly, and Theresa's hands stilled.

Belinda leaned across the table. "Do you think you'd still be friends if you'd made better choices?"

"Definitely."

"Were the choices worth it?"

Theresa glanced around the other girls as if afraid to speak her mind.

"We need to be honest with each other, and with ourselves," Belinda added.

Theresa knitted half a row without answering, as if considering the question. "At first, I thought it was worth it. I was having fun and making new friends."

"Yeah, me," Cricket said with a laugh. "Might have been your first mistake."

"No, I'm glad you're my friend. But I wish I hadn't gone so crazy. It wasn't worth it."

"Crazy's good sometimes," Zaria said. "You know, to keep life exciting. Especially when you have a boring family who won't let you do anything and expects you to be perfect."

"Well, my family doesn't trust me now. My mom hardly speaks to me. My dad won't look at me. And my ex-boyfriend still won't leave me alone. He was a *definite* mistake."

Cricket shivered as if creeped out. "Yeah, talk about scary."

"So are you trying to rebuild trust with your parents?" Lilly asked—she who now had no relationship at all with her parents. "Because, believe me, if you have parents who care about you, then it's worth it for you to make the effort."

"Didn't yours care?" Cricket looked stricken, ready to cry for Lilly.

"I guess they did in their own way. Most of the time, though, they were too wrapped up in their own drama."

"I'm sorry." Theresa reached across the table and squeezed Lilly's arm. "My parents say they love me. I guess I should try."

Evette threw down her needles and yarn. "Y'all just need to grow up. Accept that you can't change your parents' opinion of you. They're always going to expect the worst." She stalked away.

Belinda inclined her head toward Evette as a silent hint to Lilly. *Great. She thinks I can do something.* All she'd managed so far was to discourage the girl. But she got up and went to find her. Located her beside Daniel and Vera.

"I vote for the purple yarn," Evette said, her opinion obviously unsolicited.

Vera eyed the teen with the wild red hair and short leather skirt over polka-dot tights. Then Vera puffed up—shoulders thrown back, chin tilted up to look at Evette through the bottom of her bifocals. "Who are you?"

Daniel gestured to the girl. "Vera, this is Evette. She's taking a class with Lilly and Belinda."

"Um, Evette," Lilly said, "why don't you come back over to the group?"

Evette shrugged. "Whatever."

Vera's eyes narrowed at the girl's disrespectful tone. She slowly drew her attention back to Lilly. "Before you go, which do you think I should choose? The purple or the blue?"

Lilly glanced at Daniel, who patiently examined each color as if truly interested. She almost laughed out loud but caught herself. "The purple, I think."

"Me, too," Daniel said as if hoping Vera would finally settle on something…anything.

Evette snorted a laugh as she walked away. Loud laughter broke out in the gathering area and quickly faded to chatter.

Vera glared at Evette's back. "I'll take the blue. And, Lilly, if you want a thriving business, I suggest you think twice about allowing these—" she wrinkled her nose, repulsed "—rude teenagers to overrun the place." She leaned closer to Lilly to whisper. "Did you see the one in that low-cut top and skintight jeans?"

"Vera, these girls have signed up for a class," Lilly said. "A class I need to get back to, if you'll excuse me."

Vera handed Daniel three skeins of blue yarn. Then she looked down her nose at Lilly. "I gave your business card to three more of my friends. I hope they'll experience the cozy, classy place I experienced here in the past."

Daniel's jaw muscles flexed. "Ma'am, these young ladies and the boys are here as part of a ministry of the church."

"Well, ministry or not, I expect a business to cater to its paying customers."

What could Lilly say to that without alienating Vera? She grimaced and hoped it passed for a smile. "I'll see you for class tomorrow. Thanks for shopping with us."

She hoped she hadn't made a mistake. Because their ministry might scare off all the new customers, the same customers who were finally making the business profitable—and were her ticket to being able to sell the shop and head back to Kentucky to launch her new career.

Her heart hurt at the thought of leaving. Like it always had when her parents said it was time to move again.

Only this time the pain was different. Because she knew, even if she made the decision to stay in Corinthia, Daniel would eventually leave.

Had the sharing of feelings…and a kiss…been a mistake? Would it only make it more difficult to leave when the time came?

She had to prepare mentally—and emotionally—

to follow through with her goal of carrying out Aunt Talitha's wishes. To hope for anything beyond that was asking for disappointment and, as Jenna had said, for heartache.

"That was quite a grand opening," Daniel said to Lilly as he closed the folder of food pantry vouchers, pleased with the response.

"Seems like everything went well." Lilly stretched and rubbed her back. She'd worked hard the past two hours, helping visitors to the food pantry select their items. Then sometimes carrying the items to their car or bicycle.

He glanced around the small, somewhat dilapidated building. A larger church had provided it for them to use for two hours twice a week to hand out food to the needy, and he was thankful. "Appleton's about twice the size of Corinthia. Having this new food pickup location in addition to the one we opened a few months ago in our community will serve a lot more people closer to where they live."

"I'm a little surprised at the turnout," she said. "I thought it would take a while for word to get out."

"Word of mouth for this type thing travels like wildfire."

She crossed her arms in front of her and looked up at him almost shyly. "You did a good job organizing the distribution process. If we can get enough volunteers to work, it'll be a huge success."

We? She was now including herself in the church membership. Something that made him ridiculously happy. "We have a core of active, committed members for all our projects. I appreciate you signing up to help."

"You know, I've been thinking and praying about where to be involved in the ministries of the church. But it just now hit me that it's probably time for me to come down front and officially join."

He leaned toward her, brushed her hair behind her ear, questioning this crazy relationship of theirs. A relationship that left him wondering about their future. "Everyone will be happy about that. Me especially."

He dragged himself away from her, leaned back in his chair and let out a satisfied sigh. He looked into Lilly's eyes and thought she felt it, too. "You know, this is the last item I had on my list of goals for the church."

Her expression fell. She glanced away. "So what does that mean?"

A weight suddenly pressed on his chest. Had the time to leave come sooner than expected? "Well, this place has been opened one day and cleared the shelves. Looks like we'll be busy collecting donations for next week."

She jumped up as if she had rockets on her feet. "Then we should celebrate. Maybe with lunch?" She reached for his hands and pulled him out of his seat.

He tried not to show his surprise. "Sounds good. Let's lock up and—"

"Hello? Anyone still here?" Daniel's dad called from the front door.

"Over here."

"Oh, there you are," Blake said as he strode across the room. "I thought I'd stop by and see how your distribution went."

Daniel was surprised for the second time that day.

"We had a great day, Mr. Foreman," Lilly said. "Gave out all the food and will have to step up donations to meet the demand."

"Sounds like it was successful, then," he said. "As long as you can keep it stocked."

"Dad, we were about to grab lunch. You want to join us?"

"I…uh, no thanks," he stuttered. "But I did want to speak to you for a minute, Daniel."

"I'll head to the back room and straighten up," Lilly said before slipping quickly away, leaving him with his father.

Blake leaned toward Daniel as if to keep from being heard. "I actually came by to take you to out to eat, but I don't want to intrude on your date."

"Take me to lunch?"

"I'd like to talk to you sometime about…well, about how God's working in my life."

"Tell me now. I have a minute."

"No, I don't want to keep you from Lilly."

"Dad, come on…"

"God's been convicting me." He stuffed his hands in his pockets, a gesture that reminded Daniel of himself. "I've been hard on you, son. Pushing you toward what I considered success." He raised his chin, ground his teeth, obviously uncomfortable. "And I regret it. I'm sorry I didn't support you when you felt called into the ministry."

Daniel worked to keep his expression neutral, when in reality, his jaw nearly dropped open. "Thanks, Dad. I appreciate you telling me."

Blake shook Daniel's hand. "Enjoy your date." He took off toward the door as if he couldn't get away fast enough. Either playing matchmaker or embarrassed for sharing about his faith.

He caught up with Blake at the door. "We're not dating, we're simply—"

"Come on. Don't tell me you're still ignoring the fact that something's going on between you and Lilly."

Their kiss had definitely confirmed the connection. So had their conversations and shared interests. "I did acknowledge I have feelings for her. But I also have to acknowledge we're two people heading in different directions."

"That's hogwash."

"She has plans for a future in Kentucky. And I have my calling."

"Your calling shouldn't keep you from settling down, marrying, starting a family. You can serve

God here." He said it with surety, as if he'd heard it from God Himself.

"Of course I can. But I think God is calling me to something else. I've always planned to be a church starter."

"Maybe God called you to start only one church—a church that needs you. And I think Lilly needs you, too."

Couldn't his dad understand? Daniel didn't want *anyone* to need him. Because then he might need her, as well. "Did GranAnn put you up to this?"

"No. I see the situation with my own eyes." He shook his head. "Despite what you might think, I want you to be happy, son. I don't know Lilly well yet, but I see how she cares about you. And I'd hate to see you make a bad decision, especially one that could affect your whole future."

"It's not a decision. Starting churches is something I feel led to do."

"Are you sure fear isn't leading you?" Blake asked before turning and walking out. Leaving Daniel to wonder if maybe his dad could be at least partially right.

Was he really following God's will? Or was he acting out of fear of getting too attached?

No. He couldn't be that mistaken. He needed to pray for strength. Because he knew what he needed to do. With Lilly's need for stability, for a permanent home, his plan didn't—and couldn't—involve her.

# Chapter Ten

"And then this really cute guy asked me out." Zaria passed around her cell phone to show them his photo, trying to look cool, eyes shining with excitement.

"Right there on the beach?" Cricket squealed.

"Yep. But would you believe my parents wouldn't let me go?"

"Duh," Evette said. "He was, like, a total stranger, cute or not."

The girls had their regular meeting the day before but had shown up for extra work time to try to finish their knitting projects.

"Nice work, girls," Lilly said. "Theresa, you'll be finished before I will. And I started on my scarf weeks before you did."

"Um, Lilly…this is my second one." Theresa and the girls had a good laugh about that fact.

Lilly pretended to be offended, then burst out

laughing herself. "By the way, I sent off those photos I showed you—the ones of y'all—to that magazine."

"Ooh, do you think we'll be famous?" Cricket asked.

"You're already famous in my book. Look at this beautiful knitting."

She hung out with the girls for a while, though she was acutely aware that Daniel was just across the shop.

April had settled in, and as the heat outside intensified, she'd decided the shop needed a new, less drafty door so her air-conditioning wouldn't have to work so hard. Daniel had volunteered to do the job and enlisted the boys to help.

Lilly left the girls chatting about their recent spring break activities and headed to the front of the store to see how the work was going. They'd gotten the old door off its hinges and were trying to figure out how to hang the new one.

Daniel stood off to the side, allowing them to work together to accomplish their task. She slipped up beside him, pressing her arm against his. "How's it going?"

His intense gaze acknowledged their closeness in a way that made her want to lean in, to nuzzle his neck....

"Going a little slow," he said, pulling his attention to the door. "Sorry we're blocking your entrance."

"That's okay. I'm enjoying the fresh air." She got a glimpse of the azalea bushes the guys had planted, now exploding with color. Lilly glanced at her watch—nearly time for class to start.

"No, dude. It goes this way," Ian said to Dag as he impatiently pushed him aside.

"Let him do it," Parker said in defense of the newest member of their group. "He won't learn if you shove him away."

"And you won't learn if you stand there with your finger up your nose."

"You guys need to keep it down over there," Evette called.

Parker got in Ian's face. "I'm tired of you treating me like I'm an idiot."

Brave, considering Ian was a half a foot taller and a whole lot tougher. Then again, Parker had two older brothers.

Lilly glanced at Daniel to see if he would step in.

Daniel's muscles tensed. "Cut it out, guys."

Movement caught Lilly's eye.

*No. Why hadn't she seen the car?* Vera climbed the front stairs with her perfectly coiffed hair and perfectly tailored clothes and—

And with her three perfectly perturbed friends, members of their class, on the steps below her.

"Excuse me," Vera snapped. "Could we please get by?"

Ian stepped to the side and stared at Vera through squinted eyes. Not exactly friendly.

"Oops, sorry," Ricky said to the women as he

gave Parker a push out of the way. "We're replacing the door."

Parker, whose face was flushed and who apparently still didn't want to back down from Ian, gave Ricky a two-handed shove that nearly sent him flying off the porch. "Don't you be a jerk, too."

Ricky came flying back at Parker but stopped inches away. "I'm just trying to help the ladies get through the door. You need to chill."

Parker huffed out air like a bull about to charge. "I think you probably needed to chill before you got Cricket pregnant."

Lilly barely registered the comment before Ricky was on Parker and had him lifted up by the shirt, back pressed against the building.

Her heart slammed against her ribs as, a split second later, Daniel held them pried apart. "Parker, downstairs, now," he barked. "Ricky, wait inside." He nodded to Ian and Dag. "You two, stick around to help me finish this door."

As Daniel finished giving orders, the girls arrived to see what had happened. Cricket reached out for Ricky, but he shook his head and strode inside.

Evette scowled at the women as if it were their fault the guys went off. "Come on everyone, freak show's over."

Daniel ground his teeth together, his own cheeks streaked with color from having to dive into the middle of brawling teenage boys. He turned to Vera and her friends. "Ladies, I'm terribly sorry you had to witness this. The boys will be held accountable. You can be assured it won't happen again."

Time for more damage control. "I think it might be best if we cancel class today." Lilly quickly ushered them to their car.

Ann and Flo, who'd arrived sometime during the debacle, joined them.

"I'm so sorry this happened," Lilly said. "We have a ministry for these kids, kids who've made some bad decisions or have gotten into trouble, kids who merely have an awful home situation. I promise you today's fight is an anomaly. The boys are kind and usually well behaved."

Ann's brows drew downward with worry. "I'm sure Lilly's right. But it probably is best that we cancel today."

"You won't be charged," Lilly added.

Flo waved off the situation. "We understand that things happen."

"It's frightening to think you'd let those hoodlums continue to come to your place of business," Vera said, her blond hair quivering as she punctuated each word. "What if the pastor hadn't been here today?"

"I honestly think Ricky would have ended the fight if Daniel hadn't stepped in. He's a new Christian and is trying hard to be the man God wants him to be," Lilly explained.

Something flapping in the distance caught Lilly's eye. Evette waving from the porch to get their attention.

"Hey," Evette yelled. "The dudes are actually pretty decent. Not delinquents or anything. So don't hold it against Lilly."

Daniel appeared on the porch with the other teens and urged them down the stairs into the parking lot.

Lilly shook her head as the group headed their way, touched they wanted to help.

Flo happily waved at Evette as if she'd already forgiven them.

Lilly liked Flo for that ability to let things roll off her back. It was a gift, a trait she'd always admired but, always being the new girl, had never had a chance to develop. She sometimes wished she didn't care what people thought of her—what clothes she wore or how much her hair frizzed.

Daniel and the kids bravely approached.

"We came to apologize," Parker said, his eyes wide, scared. "It was my fault for losing my temper."

Vera jammed her key at the door lock, unable to get it in on the first two tries. "Lilly, I have to respectfully request that you ask those boys to leave and not come back during business hours. You have to think of your customers' comfort and safety."

Two of Vera's three friends nodded their agreement. The third looked too embarrassed to speak up. Whether she was embarrassed over the fight or over Vera's request made in front of the teenagers, Lilly couldn't tell.

"I'm sorry you feel that way," Lilly said to Vera and company, determined to maintain her own temper. "But, respectfully, I'm going to allow them to stay."

Daniel's eyebrows headed toward his hairline.

"You see," she continued, "my church wanted to help these young ladies and gentlemen make a fresh start. Like God is allowing me to make a fresh start in Corinthia." *My church.* It felt so good to say that. "But along the way, they've become my friends." She smiled at them, hoping they didn't feel like projects but like partners. "I care about them. *We* care about them."

"I'd think you'd be worried about your business first and foremost." Vera's key finally slid in the lock. "And about the reputation of your church in this town."

Lilly sought Daniel like a heat-seeking missile. "Daniel has believed in these kids from the beginning. And I fully support him. I think Corinthia will be better for it."

Daniel grinned.

Vera calmly slid into her car. "Looks like you've made your choice of who you want around your shop."

Lilly put a hand on Ann's shoulder, giving it a little squeeze of reassurance. "No, not a choice. I hope you'll stay in the class. We can all work together and form a strong community."

"I'm all for that," Flo said.

"Me, too," said Ann.

"Me, three!" Evette said, trying to look serious. But Lilly knew it was a smart remark.

She gave Evette a censuring look. "Girls, time to go finish those scarves if you plan to sell them."

Vera mumbled, "Come on, ladies. That yarn store with the noisy coffee shop is looking better by the moment." She slammed her door. As soon as her friends were settled in the car with her, she revved the engine and then rolled down her window. "I'll make sure everyone I know finds out how poorly we've been treated here."

No one said a word as Vera gunned the engine, punctuating her exit with spewing gravel.

Ian chuckled. "Better go rake the gravel again."

"That was awesome," Evette said. "I've never had anyone take up for me that way."

Lilly was glad Evette felt affirmed. But she couldn't be happy at the moment. "That was a disaster is what it was."

Jenna, who'd apparently come out behind Daniel and the teens, let Will down but held on to his hand. "Vera and her friends and coworkers make up a big chunk of our business. No offense, kids, but Lilly needs to do whatever she has to do to get them back." She glared at Daniel.

The kids didn't seem to hear her. "Man, that was amazing," Ian said. "You were like a mother bear."

"Yeah," Cricket said. "We didn't know you cared about us so much."

Theresa threw her arms around Lilly's neck. "Thank you."

As the teens gathered around, fist bumping her and each other, Lilly looked for Daniel.

He stood a few feet apart from them. The way he looked at her, his eyes shining approval, made her feel...important, cherished, like she mattered.

*That's what love looks like.*

The fleeting thought arrowed through her mind and lodged in her heart with a twinge of pain.

Even if the thought were true, he would never act on it.


Daniel drew away from the celebrating kids trying to comfort Lilly by raving about her heroic actions and reassuring her they'd help her rebuild her customer base.

He walked toward the yarn shop, trying desperately to simply take a deep breath. To think straight. Because all he could think at the moment was that he was falling in love with Lilly Barnes. And he wanted her to always have his back.

And craziest...scariest...of all, as he'd stood there watching her with the kids, knowing how much her actions had meant to them, he'd realized he wanted her to be the mother of his children. Wanted her to love them, protect them.

To love him. Support him. And allow him to love her.

Too much. He'd started to want too much.

He ran his hand through his hair as he paced back and forth in front of the shop entrance as if checking out the flowering bushes they'd planted for Lilly. The place where, at a loss for words, she'd given him a goofy thumbs-up, like he'd done when he hadn't known what to say, either.

So many awkward moments when neither of them had felt secure enough to openly love the other.

All for good reason. Hadn't they known from the beginning that they were heading in two different directions, had differing needs?

"Daniel, is everything okay?" She stood behind him, worry showing in the way her brow came together in a little vee between her eyes.

He wanted to kiss it away. To reassure her that everything would be okay.

But would it?

He had to move on, and soon. He'd already made a commitment to the folks in Valdosta. "Yeah, I'm fine. Proud of how you handled Vera."

"You are?" She came and stood beside him, brushed her hand over a nearby azalea bush.

He stared at the flowers. Couldn't risk getting lost in those gorgeous eyes, in those lips that had tasted so sweet. He tried to look inconspicuous as he put more space between them. "Yeah, really proud. I've just got a lot on my mind right now."

Her shoulders sagged. "Oh, good. I was afraid I'd messed up with the kids."

"No, you're great with them. They love you."

When her face lit with joy, he felt as if a bus sat on his chest. He prayed that someday someone would come along, someone who would deserve her and put that smile on her face for good. Someone who could settle down and give her a secure home, a family.

He jammed his hands in his pockets. "Guess we need to get back to work on that door."

"Okay. Sure." Her head tilted as if she wanted to ask more.

Thankfully, she didn't push him.

"Ian, Dag, come try to hang this door," he called to the kids clustered in the parking lot. "Ricky, Parker, I need to see you in my office."

He nodded his goodbye to Lilly and headed around the building toward the basement. As soon as he dealt with their fighting, he'd call the church in Valdosta and give them a definite start date. Then set up a meeting with Belinda, Frank and the other church leaders.

Time to start the process of moving on. He felt it as surely as he'd felt his calling to come here in the first place.

*Lord, give me strength to do this when every fiber of my being wants to stay here and start a life with this woman.*

## Chapter Eleven

That evening, Lilly couldn't continue to ignore the tension in the air in Jenna's kitchen as they ate a carryout pizza. She had to convince her sister she'd made the right choice in defending Daniel and his ministries.

Once Jenna tucked Will in bed for the night, Lilly asked her if they could sit together at the kitchen table. "Jenna, we need to talk about what happened today."

"I already tried to talk. And you blew off my concerns."

"Look, I know today was a huge blow. But I need you to understand why those kids are more important to me than four hateful women who can't see beyond themselves."

"I did some tallying. Those four hateful women represent an even larger network of potential customers. So maybe you should consider *their* feelings, as well." She hopped up and carried her plate to the dishwasher.

"Those kids there today need my support."

"And I need you, too. I need you to help make a success of The Yarn Barn. And I want you to stay so we can keep it running."

"Why the change of heart about selling?"

She slammed shut the dishwasher. "Because..." Her shoulders heaved. "...I'm going to need that money to support myself and my son."

Tears streamed down Jenna's cheeks. Lilly went to her and embraced her in a hug. "What happened?"

"Ned's giving up. Today, for the first time ever, he mentioned divorce."

Lilly felt the words like a knife to her gut. Concern with yarn and knitting and mean women paled in comparison to her sister's failing marriage. "Sit, tell me what's been going on."

Lilly had been distracted, too enmeshed in her own drama to keep up with her sister. She needed to remedy that. To watch out for her own family.

As tears poured down Jenna's face, she told Lilly about her conversation with her husband that day. "And he ended up saying he can't live in limbo any longer. He's giving me one more month to agree to counseling. If I don't, he's filing for divorce."

"You two love each other like crazy. You have to do everything you can to keep the marriage together."

"But it's not that easy."

She gripped her sister's hand and gave it a tight squeeze, willing her strength into her. "Yes, it is. You agree to go to counseling. At this point, that's all you need to do." She rubbed her sister's back. "We Barnes girls are tough…and have done well coping. But it's time to quit allowing old patterns and fears to ruin your future. It's time to swallow your pride and do whatever you have to do to keep your family together."

"I don't know if I can deal with all my baggage," she whispered.

"Ned's tried over and over to work out your marriage problems. You keep pushing him away. I'd say it's time to deal with it."

Jenna laid her head in her hands and gave a big sigh. "I admit, I'm scared."

"I know you are." *I am, too,* she wanted to say. *Scared of my feelings for Daniel. Scared how badly I want to give up my dream of a byline and beg him to stay here and spend his life with me.* "I'm scared about losing my customers, but I had to choose what was right. And helping those kids is right."

"I know getting my family back together is the right thing to do." Jenna frowned. "But I don't know how to tell him I'm afraid to do the work."

"Just…say the words. Say what's on your heart."

The words Lilly wanted to speak to Daniel lay heavy on her heart, making her ache all over. Words that should probably be spoken but would always remain locked inside—that she loved him.

Though she was good at handing out advice about being brave and saying the words, she couldn't bring herself to do the same. Because she knew Daniel would never change his plans for her.

Daniel and five of his most active church members sat around one of the round tables in the basement of The Yarn Barn, a location that now felt like home to the small congregation. Ned, Frank, Belinda, Geoff and Orson, the treasurer. These were the people who'd been on board from the beginning, working tirelessly to get the new church off the ground.

They weren't happy to hear the news he planned to move on sooner than anticipated.

"I'm stunned," Belinda said. "This seems sudden."

"Well, I've said from the beginning that this day would come once I got the ministries on track. It's come sooner than even I expected. And that's thanks to the hard work of all of you."

"Daniel," Frank said in his booming voice. "We've been talking." He gestured to each person gathered. "And I speak for all of us when I say we want you to remain here permanently."

When all heads nodded their agreement, Daniel felt good, as if he'd found love and acceptance. But he couldn't give in to the temptation of falling for their affirmation instead of following what God had called him to do.

Still, for a moment he imagined what it might be like to stay on here. To work together serving this community day in and day out for years to come. To be a part of something long-term.

No. Ever since he'd gone off to college, he'd wanted to use his gifts to help people. He was an ideas man. A man with a vision to start new things. Not someone to kick back and settle into a comfort zone. "I appreciate that offer more than you know. But I feel it's time and have confirmed with the new church that I plan to arrive in May."

Lilly's green-brown eyes popped into his mind, eyes that had drawn him yet terrified him at the same time. Surely he was feeling truly called to leave and wasn't running scared like his dad had suggested.

"I don't want you to act too quickly." Belinda patted his arm like a mother would. "Don't be afraid to consider this new option we're offering. Hang around and explore other possibilities God may be providing."

He had the uncomfortable sensation that the opportunities she spoke of involved more than his role as pastor. Belinda was a perceptive woman. Maybe she knew more than she'd let on.

"Is there anything we can do to entice you to stay?" Ned asked.

Enticement resided upstairs in a kind, caring woman named Lilly. "You people are the main reason our members love to attend worship and be a part of this church. That'll continue no matter who's preaching."

"I guess we'll have to start searching for someone to replace you." Frank, who was always so jovial, had a frown on his face for the first time that Daniel could remember.

Leaving these people would hurt. An empty ache already gnawed at him. "Yes, it's time. I'll help in any way I can."

"I'd like to suggest we hire someone interim first," Belinda said. "In case Daniel changes his mind."

"That's up to y'all. But I won't change my mind. Not when God has given me my marching orders."

The inkling of doubt he'd experienced lately jabbed again. *Lord, if there's any way I'm misinterpreting Your call, You have to show me now.*

Belinda volunteered to start the search and they closed the meeting. As the others filed out, Ned pulled Daniel aside.

"God's been working. Jenna has agreed to counseling."

The huge smile on Ned's face helped ease Daniel's sadness. He clapped him on the back. "Great news."

So there was hope for the marriage, after all. Jenna would be okay. Lilly would feel good about leaving her now. He would move on, as well.

He was glad that everything was falling into place, even though the thought of leaving his congregation made his chest ache.

The thought of leaving Lilly…well, he couldn't even go there yet.

But he would have to, and soon. As soon as they found an interim pastor as his replacement.

Lilly woke at 5:00 a.m. Sunday with Daniel's name on her lips and tears on her pale pink pillowcase. She'd been dreaming about him driving away, leaving her behind. When she hollered for him to stop, he hadn't looked back.

She stared at the light filtering in behind the blinds feeling hollow, gutted. As if Daniel had carved out a piece of her and had taken it with him, leaving a gaping hole that could never be filled.

"It's only a dream," she whispered to the room. Her temporary room.

But her time in Corinthia didn't *have* to be temporary. She hadn't yet committed to joining the magazine staff. What if she and Jenna kept running the shop? Lilly could rent an apartment or buy a small house. Possibilities swirled around in her head.

What if she kept The Yarn Barn and did freelance writing and photography on the side? But no, the shop would take all her time. She would never be able to move forward in a new career if she stayed here.

*Lord, did You put these ideas in my head? I need Your guidance.*

When she couldn't lie still anymore, she got up, read her Bible and worked in her devotional book.

She'd heard Will crying during the night. Apparently Jenna and Will had slept in. So she got ready for church and drove to the shop to do some work before the service.

The support group girls had worked diligently to finish their scarves. They would all be complete in a week or so. Lilly cleared a display rack for them in the front of the shop.

Though they realized the scarves had flaws, they'd been excited about the possibility of earning income from their projects. Placing a sign she'd made for the top of the rack made her glad the girls had something to be proud of.

The door to the basement squeaked open. "Lilly, is that you I hear up here?"

"Come in, Belinda."

Lilly's good friend approached with a smile. But it didn't quite reach her eyes, didn't light her pretty face as usual. Even her normally perky bobbed hair looked droopy, almost sad.

"What's wrong?"

"Now, what makes you think something is wrong?"

"Talk to me."

Belinda's gaze traveled the room in avoidance. "The display rack looks great. The girls will be pleased."

Lilly crossed her arms and waited, giving Belinda a look that said she wouldn't be sidetracked.

Belinda finally looked Lilly in the eye and said,

"Do you care about us here in Corinthia, do you like this town?"

Lilly straightened with a start. That comment had certainly come from out of the blue. "Well...yes. I've grown to care about all of you and feel at home."

"Then stay. You obviously love this shop. You love the girls, and they love you. The boys look up to you. You've become an important part of our church, of our lives."

The urge to cry made Lilly's nose burn. She arranged the display rack just so, making the sign more visible to the front entrance, taking a moment to compose herself. "I came here with a plan. To—"

"Plans, plans," Belinda snapped, and then sighed. "Why does everyone try to plan their lives when God is in charge?"

"I never intended to come here in the first place."

Belinda's face scrunched up as if she, too, wanted to cry. "I'm sorry. I don't mean to fuss at you. I'm disappointed. I've gotten attached to you."

Lilly hugged her friend. "And I've gotten attached to you, too."

"Then stay. Keep this place, we'll teach classes together. Why leave all your friends—and family—to go back to Kentucky?"

The request was so tempting. She'd even had the thought herself that very morning. "I can't."

"Is it because you have feelings for Daniel?"

The room stilled. Lilly's pulse throbbed in her ears, and her cheeks felt as if someone had doused them with scalding water. She couldn't look away from Belinda's gaze. "Partly," she forced out, though she hated to admit she'd fallen for him.

Belinda's shoulders sagged. "I knew it."

"I'm dealing with the feelings, trying to pray and look for God's plan for my life. And once I'm gone come winter, I'll have new ventures to keep me busy."

Staying busy would keep her satisfied, wouldn't it? Surely it would help her find contentment.

The bleak picture that formed in her mind made her flinch.

Belinda rubbed Lilly's arm. "It's not going to be easy to be separated from the man you…love?"

"Yes," Lilly whispered, feeling as if the air had been sucked out of her lungs. Belinda was right. How would Lilly ever tell him goodbye? "What am I going to do?"

"Talk to him. You *have* to talk to him."

"He kissed me," she blurted as if Belinda needed to know that detail. As if she hadn't already seen the affection between them. "But afterward, there's been so much distance between us. I've tried not to let myself hope since then."

Belinda hugged her, squeezing tightly. "Then tell him how you feel. And if it doesn't work out…well, we'll be here for you."

"I'll try, I'll—"

"Belinda? Lilly?" Frank called from the bottom of the basement stairs. "Are you up there?"

"We'll be right down." Belinda gave one last squeeze. "I'll be praying for you, for wisdom and strength."

Time to face Daniel. Would he be able to read her face? Should she grab him after the service for that talk?

No, maybe she needed a day or two to plan what she wanted to say. To brace herself to bare her soul. *To prepare myself for watching him drive away?*

She headed downstairs as the music started. Maybe her imagination was working overtime, but when she said hello to Daniel, she thought he seemed distant, distracted.

Maybe he was already pulling away from her.

At the end of the service as he held up his hands asking them to rise for a final prayer, she remembered those hands caressing her cheek, lifting her chin. Hands pulling her closer so he could kiss her. Strong, sure hands. Hands that had helped the boys learn to put in a drop-ceiling, had handed out food to the needy, had held on to Will as he learned to walk.

*Lord, I don't want to leave him. I want to stay here and make a life. I want him to choose to stay...for me. Is that wrong? Is that pulling him away from his ministry, from Your will, to ask him to stay?*

As soon as Daniel said *amen,* Cricket jumped up. "We have something we'd like to say." She signaled her friends to join her at the front.

The girls had been attending services off and on. This was the first time they'd all come together.

They each pulled out a knitted scarf—Theresa, two—and held them up for the congregation to see. All were totally finished. Lilly couldn't imagine how they'd managed it so quickly.

"Lilly and Belinda have been great," Cricket continued. "Teaching us how to knit, letting us talk and deal with stuff and...well, generally vent." She peeked around the man in front of Lilly so she could see her. "And Lilly even offered to let us sell our items in the store to make income for ourselves for whatever we wanted. We thought about buying a decent coffeemaker for the store."

Several people chuckled at her comment.

"But we talked and decided we wanted to do something in honor of these ladies. We want to donate everything we made, along with other donations we've collected, to the clothes closet and food pantry."

Lilly thought her heart would burst with joy and love as those around her broke into applause.

Once the clapping died down, Cricket said, "And the next project we want to do is to knit caps for infants at the battered women's shelter."

"Come on up here, you two," Evette said in her gruff voice with tears in her eyes, her tough veneer peeled away for the first time ever.

Lilly approached the front, her heart overflowing. When Belinda, tears streaming down her cheeks, took Lilly's hand, she knew she didn't want to leave Corinthia. She'd found her home.

But would Daniel ever be a part of it?

She glanced at him off to her side. Daniel looked proud as he, too, applauded. Though he looked outwardly pleased, she saw sadness, maybe even resignation reflected in his eyes.

*He's leaving. No matter how he feels about me, he's going to leave.*

Crushed, she looked back at the group of her new friends. Belinda signaled for them to quiet and indicated for Lilly to speak.

"Belinda and I have been blessed to work with these talented and generous young women. I'm thankful Daniel had the idea to bring them together to support each other." She gazed at the girls, clustered together with tears in their eyes. "Ladies, it means the world to us that you've chosen to do this. Thank you for the honor."

As the congregation sat, she spotted Jenna in the back. Beside her stood her husband, holding Will. When Ned realized she saw them, he put his arm around his wife and gave a thumbs-up. Jenna laid her head on his shoulder.

Everything would work out for Jenna. Their love had sustained them through the separation, and with counseling, they'd be able to deal with the issues in their marriage. Happiness for her sister and family welled and at the moment managed to trump the painful thought of Daniel leaving.

As everyone dispersed, Lilly once again thanked

the girls and then hurried over to Ned and Jenna. "I'm so glad to see you sitting together."

"I've agreed to start counseling," Jenna said. "We have our first appointment this week."

"And I'm moving home today." Ned kissed his wife, a gentle loving kiss that nearly tore Lilly's heart to shreds.

Would she ever have someone care about her like that?

"God's working in both our lives," Ned said. "I'm praying I'll be obedient. I want to be more patient, a better husband and father."

"And I'm praying…" Jenna's face reddened. "Well, I'm praying again."

As Lilly watched the happy family leave the church together, the word *obedience* ran through her head over and over. That, and Daniel's sermon about the need for trusting God. Maybe God was trying to show her something.

She needed to learn to be obedient. To trust in His perfect plan. *Plan.* That morning, Belinda had complained that everyone seemed to have plans of their own instead of following God's plan.

Wasn't that what Lilly had been doing? Planning her life without a thought to God's will?

It was time she became obedient and looked to God for what He wanted. And maybe, just maybe, He was leading her to stay in Corinthia, to serve Him in this community, in this church family. To be here to support her sister. To be here to help with the ministries she'd joined.

Peace settled across her shoulders as well as deep inside her. Maybe, after years and years of feeling adrift, she was finally in the place God wanted her to be.

She had to talk to Daniel.

## Chapter Twelve

One look at Lilly's face as she stood in his office doorway, and Daniel knew he was in trouble.

She had that dreamy, happy look. Maybe it was because she, too, had witnessed the kiss Ned gave Jenna. Daniel himself had been happy to see them together. But he couldn't risk Lilly confessing any romantic feelings.

He didn't have the willpower to turn her away. "Hey, Lilly. I'm sorry to be rude, but I've got to run."

Hurt flared in her eyes. "Oh. Okay."

"Gran's expecting me. And Dad called saying I needed to get over there right away." True, but a bit exaggerated. His dad had called to tell him the pot roast was getting cold, and that he wouldn't wait much longer before diving in.

"Okay. Can I maybe drop by later?"

He couldn't look at her so instead he flipped a notepad closed, shuffled some papers. "I'm not sure. How about I call you?"

*Oh, Lord, help me do this.* Unable to be so cold-hearted, he forced himself to look her in the eye.

The corners of her mouth drew slowly upward, her expression one of understanding, hinting that she knew something he didn't. "Sure. When you're ready."

He couldn't bear it. He nodded and rushed out of his office. Drove to his grandmother's house even while praying for the strength to do what he had to do. To do what he was called to do.

"About time," his dad said as he forked a bite of beef into his mouth.

"Got here as quickly as I could," he said, trying to be nice when the tone of his dad's voice set his teeth on edge.

"What's wrong, honey?" GranAnn reached for him and pushed him into his chair. She gave his shoulders a squeeze.

"Rough day. Decisions to make—hard decisions."

"Anything I can help with?" Blake asked.

His dad's genuine expression stopped him from an abrupt refusal. "I plan to move in May. A committee at the church has started looking for an interim replacement."

Ann worried at the buttons on her dress. "No. You can't mean it."

"They're ready. I'm ready."

Blake's brows angled downward in typical disapproving fashion. "Did something happen to precipitate this?"

Daniel couldn't quite meet his dad's eyes for fear that it would be obvious that he'd messed up and fallen in love with Lilly. "No, sir. When I crossed the last item off my list of goals, I realized it was time to commit to a start date at my new church."

"You can't leave," Gran said. "I promised Talitha. We had it all worked out. You and Lilly." She blinked at tears. "Perfect for each other."

What? Shaking his head, he held up his hand to stop her. "I'm sorry, GranAnn, but you can't play matchmaker. This is my life. My calling."

"My work was my calling, too," his dad said. "I'd grown up poor, so I was determined to make a decent living to give my family everything I never had. I was sure God wanted me to be the best provider I could." He shook his head in disgust. "I let the drive to succeed rule my life."

His dad had never admitted that. Never talked about being poor or about feeling driven to provide. Daniel had assumed his dad preferred work to family life, then later, that he needed to stay busy to deal with grief.

"Dad, why didn't you ever tell me that?"

"Because I couldn't see it. I thought all I was good at was providing. Had no clue how to relate to a hurting child. Now that I've had this time with you, God's been showing me that I can be more than just a provider for my family. I want to be a part of your life."

Daniel took two short breaths, trying to hold his

emotions at bay. "I'd like that. I'm sorry that, soon, it'll be from a distance."

"Don't do it, son. Don't fall into the same trap I fell into, of assuming you know what's best instead of trusting in God's sovereign power."

He stared into his dad's eyes as he thought about all he would be giving up if he left.

Unable to eat a bite, he pushed away from the table. "I've already committed to going. If nothing else, the Foreman men are good at making a plan and following through."

As he walked away, his grandmother grabbed his arm. "I've been praying about this. I've truly felt God leading me to help bring you and Lilly together."

"Gran…"

"Don't act too quickly. Please pray about Lilly, too."

He steeled himself against the distress on her face. "I appreciate you caring about my happiness. But unless God gives me a strong direction otherwise, I'm going through with my plans."

"I'm disappointed, son," his dad said. Disappointed he wouldn't get the chance for that father-son relationship? Or disappointed in Daniel himself?

Even with the protective wall he'd tried to slam in place, the words hurt.

Lilly tried her best to remain upbeat and hopeful. But Daniel had never called on Sunday. And he'd avoided coming to the office on Monday.

On the bright side, Jenna, who'd finally decided the church wasn't out to break up her family, came that day to help with customers so Lilly could work with Belinda and the girls. She didn't know for sure how many customers showed up, but it sounded like a good number. Business seemed to be picking up despite anything negative Vera shared around town.

Maybe that had something to do with the fact that each of the teen boys and girls considered it a matter of personal honor to win the shop at least four good customers.

Another positive was the huge donation of food and clothes the girls had brought that filled the back of Zaria's SUV. As they'd transferred it to Lilly's car, she was blown away by the abundance of items they'd collected at school and around their neighborhoods to go along with their scarves. Their excitement was contagious.

The girls drove away, all but Cricket, who stood out front waiting for Ricky to give her a ride home.

"You sure you don't want me to run you by your house?" Lilly asked.

"No, I want to spend some time with Ricky." She fidgeted, bit her lip. Then she let out an ear-piercing, happy squeal. "I can't hold it in any longer. Ricky proposed!" She flashed her left fingers and wiggled them, a tiny diamond solitaire announcing their commitment to the world.

"What?" She grabbed Cricket's hand, and thought the girl would break bones, her grip was so tight.

"He asked my mom and dad for my hand in marriage, all formallike. And they agreed! But only after we both graduate from high school. And we have to get good grades. And they'll let him come to my house any time as long as we promise to wait until we're married to…well, you know…" She sucked in a long, deep breath. "And we have to promise to finish college or technical school so they don't have to support us forever."

Lilly's laughter bubbled out, along with the strong desire to squeal like Cricket. "So what did you say when he asked?"

"Well, duh! What do you think?" She nearly doubled over giggling, as much as she could bend with a baby in the way, anyway.

Lilly hugged the girl and held tight. Nice to see things looking up in a situation that nearly ended in tragedy.

"It won't be easy," Lilly felt compelled to say.

"Oh, I know. Believe me. We're way too young to be starting a family, especially knowing our baby could have problems. But we're willing to take the bad with the good, to make it work."

Ricky came around the building then, pure happiness beaming on his face as he looked at his future wife. "Oh, man, you told her? I thought we were going to wait and tell everyone together."

"It just popped out of me," Cricket said.

He shook his head and laughed, then nodded

toward his truck. "Come on, time to take you home to study."

"Congratulations, Ricky," Lilly said. She was smiling so big, it felt as if her eyes were squinted shut.

His Adam's apple bobbed. "I owe you a lot. You helped me step up."

"You'll do a fine job."

With a jerky motion, he threw his arms around her. The awkward hug only lasted a moment before he grabbed his fiancée's hand and took off across the parking lot.

She swiped at tears as they drove off. Then she forced her emotions into check so she could make her deliveries.

She dropped the scarves and clothes at the clothes closet in Corinthia. Then she headed with the food to the new food pantry in Appleton.

There, in the back lot, sat Daniel's car.

Her heart flittered, and her stomach seized into a nervous knot. *Please give me the words,* she prayed. And since he'd successfully avoided her the other day, preventing her from sharing her feelings, she added, *And if it's in Your will for me to have this talk with him, then please make him a captive audience.*

A spark of hope made laughter bubble out of her for the second time that afternoon. She carried the first load inside and nearly chuckled at the way Daniel's eyes widened when he saw her. The man did not want to have this conversation. He didn't realize, though, she and Belinda had been praying for it since Sunday.

"Oh, hi, Lilly."

"I brought the donations from the girls."

"Oh…uh…great." After a few awkward seconds, he seemed to come to his senses and hopped up. "I'll help you."

When they'd finished stacking the food on shelves, he stuffed his hands in his pockets and glanced around the room as if trying desperately not to look at her.

Her heart stuttered when she realized Daniel was scared, plain and simple. Scared of what she would tell him. She nearly lost her courage. What if he outright rejected her admission? What if he didn't feel the same way?

But then she remembered her prayers and the sense of peace she had about her decision to stay in Corinthia. Surely, God was leading her on this scary, new path.

She reached out and lightly touched his arm. "Daniel, I want—"

He jerked away as if she'd stung him. "I should go up front in case anyone else comes in."

As if on cue, the front door creaked opened.

The relief in his expression sparked irritation, giving her the gumption she needed. "You're going to have to talk to me at some point."

"Let me help this person first."

Instead of biding her time, she jumped in to pack

up the food the guest requested. Which sped the process and left Daniel no choice but to listen to her once the man had left.

As soon as the door closed, she swallowed back her fear and stepped in front of him. "I was disappointed you ran from me on Sunday, as if trying to escape."

"I'm sorry I never called." He took a deep breath and stared at the ceiling. "Gran was upset I won't change my mind and stay here permanently. My dad…well, we made some progress. But he basically thinks I'm running."

"Why?"

"Says I'm afraid, that I'm making the same mistakes he made." He checked his watch, stalked across the floor and flipped over the closed sign. "How can he all of a sudden claim to regret being away all the time when I was little? How can he act as if handing out advice to me now makes him the father I always needed but never had?" He clutched at the back of a chair, his knuckles white. "Sorry. Guess I'm still angry."

His pain hurt her, a physical ache that made her want to reach out and hold him, comfort him. But touching would only complicate matters when they needed to talk.

"What happened after your mom died?"

He looked at her, his normally playful, sky-blue eyes now stormy, tormented. "He was a workaholic.

Never home. Then after Mom died, he pretty much withdrew, swamped in his own grief."

She could envision the eight-year-old version of Daniel, grieving, missing his mom, all alone without his father to depend on.

Daniel stared out a tiny window. Its frame had been painted so many times the wood looked rumpled and warped. "When I was really little, I didn't understand what was going on. But once I got older, I tried everything to make him happy, to make him smile again. I practiced football in the heat of the summer until I'd throw up, working to be the best player on the team. I studied hard to get all A's at school. To make the best score on my SAT. To date the prettiest girls. To get a football scholarship. To get accepted to Dad's alma mater."

She clenched her hands together as his words stabbed her like knife jabs. So much pain on his face. "You were a kid," she said as if the words had been ripped out of her.

"Yeah, but I was *his* kid. And I wasn't enough."

Unable to stay away from him, she closed the distance. Wrapped her arms around his waist. "Daniel, I know what it's like to not be enough. To have parents who were too wrapped up in their own problems to notice me. To have a fiancé who had to find happiness outside our relationship. You and I have been injured, but it doesn't have to define us."

He brushed back her hair from her face but didn't speak, his eyes reflecting his turbulent thoughts.

Maybe what he thought was his calling wasn't really a calling from God, but more a crutch to keeping him from working through his fears.

The thought made perfect sense and explained his actions. Hope blossomed. She had to tell him how she felt, to reassure him.

She put her hand on his cheek. "We can get past this, move on. To our future."

His wall of defense slammed into place and was palpable.

"Daniel, don't shut me out."

"If we continue this conversation, it will only make my leaving more painful. And I *am* going to leave." He pulled out of her arms, stalked to the back room and opened the door leading out to their cars. "You and I both know that no matter how much we care about each other, our lives will soon head in two directions."

How could she ever let him know she loved him if he'd never listen? She rushed around him, shut the door and leaned against it, blocking the exit.

Panic hit Daniel full force. He had to get away from Lilly. She made him waver. Made him want. Made him long for things he couldn't have.

He raked his fingers through his hair, mainly to keep from running them through the luxurious curls that spilled over her shoulders and practically called his name. "Please let me leave."

"You're going to hear me out."

"No, I'm not. I'm going to—"

She placed her hand over his heart. He froze. By the time he came to his senses, she'd gripped his shirt and pulled him closer. "You're going to hear me out before I lose my nerve."

"Lilly, don't. It's already arranged. I'm moving to Valdosta."

Her arms snaked around his waist, wrapping him in her warmth, in her soft flowery fragrance. "You see, that's the problem." She rose up on her toes and stared at his lips. "I don't want you to leave. I want you to stay here, with me."

His pulse pounded in his ears as he tried to back away. But his feet refused to budge, mired in his indecision. She stared into his eyes, though, inviting him without words to stay right where he was, in the circle of her arms. And right then, he wanted that. Wanted to feel secure and happy.

As he'd feared, he had no willpower to leave her. He wanted to stay here and love her. To make a life with her.

"I can't fight this," he whispered as he cupped her face and ran his thumbs over her cheeks. He backed her against the door, closing the space between them. When his lips finally met hers, she sighed and melted into him, as if she'd finally accomplished what she'd set out to do.

And he loved it. He was glad of it at this moment. Glad she'd forced him to face the truth.

He deepened the kiss, pouring all the love he'd

been holding back, all the love he'd wanted to give but hadn't allowed himself to. He scattered kisses on her cheeks, her temples. Along the soft curve of her jaw to just below her ear. Words of love formed on his lips and almost slipped out. "You're so beautiful," he whispered.

Her head fell back, and he trailed kisses to the hollow of her neck.

"I love you, Daniel."

He plowed his hands into her hair and kissed her again, craving the feel of her soft lips, the taste of her…. But the words she'd spoken dragged him back to reality.

*Too far. This has gone too far.*

They couldn't be together. Loving her was dangerous. At best, he'd uproot her over and over, making her unhappy. At worst, she'd end up resenting their life together and leave him.

He pulled away, trying to catch his breath. "This can't happen again."

"I've decided to stay in Corinthia. To make a life here." Why wasn't she as breathless as he was? She sounded calm, assured.

He tried to back away, but she tightened her arms around him.

"I feel God wants me here, and I think maybe He brought us together." A heated blush stole across her cheeks.

He ran his finger over the pinkness, one last touch. "God's calling me away. You've known that all along."

"I'm learning to trust God's plan for my life, to give up control." She lifted to her toes again and kissed one corner of his mouth then the other. "I want you to trust me with your heart."

Like someone injecting him with a dose of reality, ice water ran through his veins.

The shock gave him the power to step away. "I'm sorry, Lilly. I care about you, and I've enjoyed working with you. But I can't let romantic feelings keep me from my dream of helping people."

She put her hands on his shoulders. "Look at how you've helped Ricky and Ian and Cricket."

The warmth of her hands made him wish...just maybe... *No.* "I'm leaving no matter how badly I'd like to stay with you."

"Don't you see? God brought us together for a reason. To serve this church and this community together. Look what we've accomplished already."

Her smile broke his heart. And he now had to break hers. "I've talked to the church leaders, and Belinda's already looking for my replacement. I've committed to the church in South Georgia. I start in May."

Her hands slid down his arms and fell to her sides. The hurt on her face made him sick at his stomach. He reached out....

She flinched. "What do you mean, you've committed?"

He opened the door, knowing full well she would leave and probably never speak to him again.

"They've signed a lease for a place for the new church to meet. And I've given them my word that I'm coming."

She sucked in a breath. Stared at him as if he was the lowlife she first thought him to be, back when she'd accused him of being like her dad. The way she would look at him every day of their lives if he selfishly asked her to marry him and be a part of his ministry.

"I thought you felt the same." Her eyes pooled with tears.

He gritted his teeth until they hurt, knowing he had the words to ease her pain. But he locked them inside, looking into her eyes, wishing there was another way.

She looked away. "Have you considered asking me to go with you?"

The request sent a shock wave through his body. "And have you grow to hate me for uprooting you over and over? No. I'm sorry. So sorry."

How was he going to pretend she didn't love him? Worse yet, how was he going to pretend he didn't love her more than he'd ever loved anyone before?

Some of the fight returned to her eyes, enough to carry her out the door. And out of his life.

## Chapter Thirteen

*Breathe. Hold it together.*

But Lilly couldn't. She couldn't even see to drive.

She pulled over to the side of the road and swiped at the tears, angry at them for falling when she'd tried so hard to keep them at bay.

Stupid, so stupid. How could she have let herself fall for Daniel, even when she'd known from the beginning he was the type who wouldn't put down roots. He and his big ideas for ministries all over the state. He and his big ideas for starting new churches.

As if each one would be a notch on his belt in heaven.

Anger mixed with the hurt, swirling inside until she wanted to scream and spew it all out, to rage at him and hurt him in some way.

She threw her head against the headrest, closed her eyes and squeezed tightly.

She would not cry one more tear over the man. If he didn't want her, she couldn't make him.

She sniffed, gave her eyes one last swipe and grabbed her cell phone to call Belinda. Before she could, it buzzed, a call from her magazine-owner friend in Kentucky. "Hey, Gloria."

"Hey, girl! How's Georgia?"

She fought a sob. "Not too great at the moment."

"I'm sorry. I hope my news will perk you up."

"News?"

"I want to publish your article on the girls' knitting group. The shots are outstanding."

"I thought that's what we're meeting to discuss in July."

"It was. But I want it sooner. In July, we'll talk about having you intern with us once you move back."

An internship? *Lord, thank You for this encouragement.* "Wow, Gloria. This is an amazing opportunity."

"I'll keep in touch by email, will send waivers. Go ahead and get permission from the girls and their parents. Can't wait till you get back home to Louisville for good."

Yes, home, in Kentucky. Where she belonged. Where she wouldn't have to look at the basement door of The Yarn Barn and think of Daniel and how much she missed him. Where she'd have a nice quiet life, safe from heartache and disappointment. A life where she could follow her dreams.

One dream, anyway.

She signed off with Gloria and pulled the car back on the road.

No more pity party. Time to get back on track with her original plan—to put all her efforts into growing the yarn business, readying it to put on the market.

She drove to Jenna's, thrilled to see Ned's truck in the driveway. Inside, she heard laughter in the kitchen. The perfect family portrait met her: husband holding his baby, spooning food into his mouth. Wife standing at his shoulder with her hand on him possessively, lovingly. Husband looking up at wife with adoration.

Everything Lilly had ever wanted but never dared to hope for.

And now it was once again out of her reach.

She pulled herself through the doorway and pressed her face against the cool wall of the dark living room. *Lord, help me through this. I guess I got everything wrong. Show me a new picture of what my life will be like. I'm trusting You and only You. I'm in Your hands.*

She hated to interrupt the reunion scenario with a request to talk to Jenna. She would go to her room and wait until morning.

Then tomorrow, she would let Jenna know she wanted to sell The Yarn Barn. And that she planned to put word out it was going on the market, maybe get a buyer lined up now.

The end of her one-year sentence couldn't get here quickly enough.

\* \* \*

Daniel looked at the interim pastor's résumé that Belinda had left on his desk two days earlier. It looked good. The guy was coming in a couple weeks to preach and meet everyone. Daniel needed to arrange a time to tell the kids what was going on before they heard from someone else.

He shut his eyes and blocked the pain. He'd avoided thinking about what had happened the previous week. Had gone once again into avoid-Lilly mode.

Apparently, she'd done the same. He'd only seen her at a distance on Sunday. He hadn't gone into the shop at all. And she hadn't ventured downstairs.

Footsteps approached. "Got a minute?" Belinda looked concerned.

"Sure."

She plopped down in the chair. "We've got a problem."

Images of bounced checks or dissatisfied church members zipped through his mind. "What's going on?"

"Lilly and Jenna have decided to sell the shop, and they've put out word, looking for potential buyers."

*No. Surely she wouldn't do that.* He opened his mouth to ask why. But then he snapped it shut. "How's that a problem for *us?*"

Belinda raised a brow at him—the motherly, disapproving look she seemed to give him more often lately.

"I'm serious. I don't think selling the shop is a good idea, but unless the new owner kicks us out, the sale has nothing to do with us."

"It has everything to do with *you*."

He slumped in his seat. Apparently Belinda knew what happened. "So she told you?"

"She hasn't told me anything. I gathered she's either running away out of fear, or she's reacting to your leaving."

Belinda had enough of the story. "I hate the thought of her leaving, but I don't have any right to ask her to stay. She's your friend. You should try to persuade her.

"Maybe between the two of us…" Her expression, a mix of threat and pleading, made him waffle.

Belinda was right, of course. Last week, she'd talked about both of them staying. If she was planning to leave now then he was responsible. He needed to at least try to do something. "I'll see what I can do."

She left, and he tried to think of some way to prevent Lilly from selling. The shop made her happy. It gave her a sense of community she'd wanted and had missed all of her life.

He stood and paced his tiny office. Surely she'd regret selling. She'd move away and then miss all her new friends. She'd want to come back, but someone else would own the shop.

Unless…

Unless someone bought it and held it in safekeeping until she changed her mind.

He couldn't do it alone. But he knew someone who could help.

Daniel stood on his dad's front porch for the first time ever. Strange he hadn't visited since his dad had retired and moved to Corinthia months before.

But then, until lately, that's the way their relationship had always been. Distant. Tense. Combative.

He knocked, anyway. After a couple minutes, he assumed his father wasn't home. But then the door opened.

Blake's mouth gaped. "Daniel?"

"I need your help."

For a split second the man seemed confused. Then he pulled the door wide-open. "Of course. Come in."

Daniel followed his father through a fancy entry hall into a plush office with rich cherry paneling and a massive wooden desk. The room was reminiscent of his dad's office in Daniel's childhood home and sent him whirling back to the times he'd tried to talk to his dad as he hunched over his desk. The times he'd tried to tell him of one achievement or another, hoping it would bring his father back to him, would make him proud.

"Have a seat and tell me what you need."

"I need you to help me buy The Yarn Barn."

"What?" He flopped back in his chair and stared at his son.

"Lilly's talked Jenna into putting it on the market. They're taking offers now and will sell as soon as they've fulfilled the year-long requirement of their aunt's will."

"Is she going back to Kentucky?"

He couldn't speak past the football-size lump in his throat. Maybe sitting across a desk from his dad made him feel like a kid again. Or maybe the thought of Lilly two states away put the lump there. "Yes. And I think she'll regret selling. I'd like to buy it anonymously and hold it in safekeeping until she changes her mind and returns."

His dad's shoulders slumped. His face fell. "You care that much about her."

Daniel nodded.

"You know the better solution would be for you to stay here. Continue your ministry where people have come to love you and depend on you. I imagine Lilly would stay, as well."

She would have. But not now that he'd pushed her away. "I'm already committed to go. I'm doing what I need to do."

"So you're determined, then?"

To leave? Yes. But he was determined to protect Lilly, too. He knew without a doubt she would miss her life in Corinthia, would change her mind. He wanted her to have this loving community to fall back on. "Yes, sir. I am. I have savings, but I can't afford it myself."

As his father considered the request, he stared at

Daniel. Disapproval, maybe even disappointment flickered in his eyes.

Then he opened a drawer and pulled out his checkbook. "Tell me how much you need."

## Chapter Fourteen

"We have a buyer." Lilly had wanted to ease into the conversation with Belinda but didn't know how to say the words that would separate her from her church, her friends, from everything she held dear.

Belinda's knitting needles paused, but then they continued their quick, smooth motion, a motion Lilly would never master. "For what?" she finally asked.

"You know what."

"You're making a mistake. I usually butt out, figuring the person knows her situation better than I do. But this time, I know in my bones I'm right."

Lilly slowly added a row to her scarf—a scarf she still hadn't finished, even as Cricket and the girls had whipped out a scarf or more each. But at least she'd learned. She'd gotten involved and had helped some teens along the way. And most importantly, her time in Corinthia had brought her back to her faith in God.

She'd be leaving eventually, but leaving as a

changed, better person. Even with the heartache over Daniel, she had no regrets.

She stuffed the needles into the skein of yarn and slipped it into the beautiful canvas tote bag Belinda had made. Running her fingers over the embroidery left her feeling bereft.

She should be relieved. "The buyer is offering a good price. And he—or she—is even willing to wait until the year is up."

"He or she?"

"It's an investment group."

"An investment group? Are you kidding? It could be some company that's going to plow down this place and build an apartment complex."

She'd worried about the same thing. "No. We'll have in writing that they'll keep it as The Yarn Barn. The representative for the group assured me they want to see the shop profit. They see the potential."

Belinda pleaded with her eyes. "What can I do to change your mind? You've been so happy here."

"I have been happy. And I'm going to miss you like crazy. But I'm trying to trust God's plan. The fact that we have a potential buyer so quickly, who's being flexible…well, to me that's confirmation I'm on the right track." She reached for Belinda's hand and gave it a squeeze. "Will you come visit me?"

"Of course. And I'll look forward to you coming home for holidays."

*Home.* The word made her chest ache. Still, God

was in control. She had to trust Him. God would come through, would put her where she could best serve Him.

The guys Daniel mentored sat around the table working hard on their studies. Daniel would miss spending time with them, miss watching them bond, mature, grow into the men God wanted them to be.

He clapped his hands and rubbed them together. "How about a break?"

They looked up, surprised. Daniel didn't usually let up on them. Today he'd make an exception. He had to tell them the news he was leaving.

"You kiddin'?" Ian asked.

"Nope. Let's go upstairs and see if the girls are about done with their class. Maybe we can all head outside and enjoy this beautiful weather."

Ricky raised a brow at him like he thought he'd lost it.

The others hopped up, ready to ditch the books.

They pounded up the stairs ahead of Daniel, which suited him fine. He didn't relish facing Lilly. *Don't look right at her. Give her some time.*

He needed to quit thinking. To go through the motions on autopilot. That's the only way he'd be able to follow through in the coming weeks.

"Yo!" Ian called as he burst through the door first. "The jailer has let us out. Time for a break."

Giggles echoed along the stairway as Daniel stepped into the room. And looked right at Lilly.

She appeared tired. Stressed.

Sad.

And he was at fault.

"What's going on?" Belinda asked.

"They've been studying hard, so it's time for a break." He shoved his hands in his jeans pockets. "Plus, I wanted a minute to talk with all of you."

Belinda nodded, understanding. "It's a gorgeous day. Y'all head outside. Lilly, you, too. I'll straighten up in here."

Lilly shot Belinda a look of disbelief but followed as they headed outside. The boys and girls goofed off, teasing like siblings—except for Ricky and Cricket who held hands, swinging their arms as they walked, Cricket's engagement ring sparkling in the sun.

Daniel sat on the front steps and had them circle around. Cricket sat beside him. Lilly stood off to herself behind the group, looking wounded…resigned.

"Oh, there you are, Daniel."

He glanced beyond the teens and spotted his dad standing in the parking lot. Having to share this news was difficult enough. He didn't need his dad standing by, disapproving.

"Hi, Dad."

"I looked for you in your office. I need you to… uh…sign some papers."

Those papers would commit their newly formed

investment company to buy the shop. He'd agreed to meet his dad and had totally forgotten.

"I'll be there soon."

His dad nodded and headed around to the back. Slowly. Too slowly.

"What's up, Preacher Dan?" Zaria asked, using the nickname she'd recently given him.

He would miss her teasing. "I have some news that I want y'all to hear first from me."

"What's up?" Evette didn't have a hint of concern on her face.

These kids trusted him.

A sick feeling started in his gut and grew until it constricted his chest.

They were strong kids, though. They'd be fine. "We've accomplished a lot since we started the church. Everything is going well. Lots of new outreach in the community."

They stared at him, nodding in agreement—except for Dag, who squatted down to mess around in the dirt.

"It's time for me to start a new ministry somewhere else."

The circle of teens stood there motionless, as if waiting for the punch line.

"A man will be coming soon to meet everyone and to preach. If it goes well, the church will hire him as an interim pastor."

Ricky leaned forward at the waist, as if Daniel had punched him. "You can't be serious."

"It's time I move on."

"Well, that doesn't make sense." Cricket gripped Daniel's shoulder. "You haven't been here long at all."

"I said from the beginning that I'm a church starter."

"Yeah, but we didn't think you'd ever really go," Parker said, his earnest blue eyes heartbreaking.

The sick knot inside him tightened. "Everyone has worked so hard, and now you're in a good place, ready for me to leave."

"Says who?" Ian's dark eyes flashed hurt before the hurt quickly morphed to anger. A look Daniel had seen on his face often in the beginning. An expression he'd rarely worn lately.

For once, Lilly didn't seem to be jumping in to support him. He couldn't blame her.

The look of anguish on her face as she glanced around the circle, watching the kids' reactions, made the moment unbearable.

"I'll miss all of you." He stood. "I'll be in my office if any of you want to talk more." He took off, following the path his dad had taken.

"No, don't let us stop you," Ian called to Daniel's back as he rounded the corner. "We wouldn't want to interrupt your *important* ministry with our stupid neediness."

For some reason, Daniel's gaze traveled to Lilly instead of to Ian.

She stood on the sidewalk, shoulders slumped,

listless. Their eyes met for a moment, his begging her to help. To do something to comfort the kids when he didn't have anything to offer.

As expected, her caretaker nature kicked in, and she put an arm around Theresa. Then she reached out and put a hand on Ian's arm. "Come on, guys. Give Daniel a break. He's doing what he feels God leading him to do."

Daniel didn't stick around to see what else she might say or do. He escaped to his office, hoping to shut himself inside.

Too late, he remembered his dad was waiting.

"Tough scene out there," his dad said.

Daniel shot his dad a censuring look.

"I couldn't help overhearing as I walked away."

"This isn't any of your business."

"It is my business. Because it's my fault."

His fault? Daniel sank into his chair, the springs squeaking their protest. "Right or wrong, none of my decisions has anything to do with you."

"If you walk away from here right now, you'll be making a mistake." Blake's gruff words were softened by his distressed expression, as if he feared he no longer had any influence over his son.

"We already discussed this at Gran's the other day."

"It's all my fault. For neglecting my family. For shipping you from pillar to post after your mom died."

"Dad…"

"That young woman out front loves you. And you're blowing it. All because of my mistakes— mistakes God has been and is still revealing to me."

Daniel couldn't bear the sorrow and regret on his dad's face. So many years of wasted time. To avoid confronting his dad's grief, Daniel leaned his forearms on his thighs and stared at the concrete floor.

He had planned to put down some kind of floor covering before leaving.

"Daniel, look at me."

He lifted his head and stared into eyes that mirrored his—the same blue, the same shape…the same sadness.

"Son, I've been wrong so many times. But God has forgiven me for the damage I've caused. And now I'd like to move forward. To help you move past it, too. Before you ruin your chance for happiness with Lilly."

"Let's not make this about Lilly. It's about me moving on to the next job, to do what I do best."

Blake grimaced and shook his head. "You have to follow your heart and trust in love despite the example I set. Don't let fear stand in your way."

"Fear? You want to talk about fear?" Anger shot through his veins, making him want to punish the man who'd checked out and left Daniel scared and alone. Did his dad think a few motivational words could make up for years of worry and feeling as if he'd failed? "How about my fear of coming home and finding you'd left for good? Or the fear of never living up to your ridiculously high expectations. Oh, and then don't forget the constant fear of letting everyone down as badly as I let you down when I couldn't pull you out of your depression."

Afraid he might say something worse, he stalked out of his office and straight out the back door. He headed into the woods, barreling blindly along a narrow path. When he reached a fallen tree, he stopped to catch his breath. He walked across the tree and sat on it, his back toward the church, his dad, his life.

Yes, Daniel was angry. His dad had deserted him when his mother died.

*And now I'm deserting Lilly. I'm no better than my father.*

He dropped his head into his hands. "I don't want to move away." There, he'd said it out loud, even if it was only to himself. He didn't want to leave Corinthia.

*Lord, have I been mistaken? Because I admit right now, I don't want to leave Lilly. It doesn't feel right to leave her, the kids, the church.*

*Have I latched onto my church-starting ministry out of fear of getting attached to people I might lose? Like some kind of lonely eight-year-old boy?*

He leaned over and grabbed a stick. Scraped away leaves and moss and rotted bits of plants, revealing the fresh, rich soil below. *Lord, help me shove away all the junk, all the baggage. Help me to see You and Your perfect will.*

For so long he'd tried to plan and do everything

on his own, thinking he was following God's will. When in reality, he was following his own will, doing what felt safe and comfortable.

*God, is it time to stick around for a while? What should I do?*

The words *wait and listen* flitted through his mind and began to take root.

"Wait and listen?"

He sat a while, hoping for a lightning bolt of insight. But nothing happened. No audible commands from God. No brilliant ideas about a new plan.

*Wait and listen.*

Well, he couldn't wait here all day. He needed to go back inside. To apologize to his dad for lashing out when his dad had been trying to change, to ask for forgiveness.

He headed up the path to return to his office and found his dad coming toward him. They stopped with a couple feet between them. A bird whistled a happy song in a nearby tree.

"I can't expect you to forget your painful childhood," Blake said. "But I'm hoping that someday you'll be able to forgive me."

Daniel had to forgive his father. God expected it. And it was time. Time to give it up and let it go if he ever wanted a chance at happiness. "I'll forgive you. With God's help." The words came easier than he expected, and left him feeling a sense of release. It wouldn't be easy to let go of the past, but forgiveness was a start.

Maybe he needed to offer the same chance to his dad. "I hope you'll forgive me for lashing out."

Blake came closer and gave Daniel's shoulder a squeeze. "Thank you. I forgive you, too." His dad gave a tentative smile. "Son, you're a good man. And I truly think God brought you and Lilly here at the same time, brought you together for a reason. Don't be afraid of loving her. Of allowing her to love you."

God had certainly changed Blake Foreman. He could change Daniel, as well—if Daniel would give control over to Him. Maybe God would equip him to be a good pastor on a permanent basis. Would equip him to be a good husband…one who could risk loving, risk staying.

He looked into his father's eyes, and for the first time felt a release from the anger. "Thank you for speaking the truth."

*Wait and listen.*

Daniel nearly gasped as he realized the gift God had given him, had given them.

"And, Dad, thank you for being here when I needed you."

Tears flooded his dad's eyes. His lip trembled. "Thank you for allowing me. I'm proud to call you my son."

Words Daniel had longed his whole life to hear. He reached out and met his father's embrace.

*Lord, strengthen me to be the man this community needs. To be the man Lilly needs. Because I listened, and it looks like I'm staying.*

## Chapter Fifteen

Lilly flipped over the page on the calendar. May had arrived. Daniel would be leaving soon.

She fought to reject the sadness, the despair. Said a quick prayer for strength. Each day was getting better. She could manage.

Lilly shut the computer, relieved to see The Yarn Barn's month had ended in the black once again. By the time she and Jenna sold the store, she could feel good about what they'd accomplished.

Looking around the shop, she witnessed the signs of a thriving community. The ancient coffeepot half-full. The various ceramic mugs regulars had left. A skein of yarn Flo had forgotten but would pick up tomorrow.

She had developed a routine. A routine she loved and would miss.

No. No time for doubt or regret. Jenna and Ned were doing better. She felt certain they'd be fine. When the time came for her to leave Corinthia, she could move on knowing she'd accomplished all she'd set out to do while here.

When she got to Louisville, she would make finding a church home a priority. New friends, new church family, new career, new life with God in charge. Yes, she could do—

The shop door opened and the bells sounded. *Oh, brother.* She'd forgotten to lock the door and flip the open sign to Closed.

She sighed as she headed that direction. "I'm sorry, but we're closed."

"I'm not here to buy anything."

Her heart surged at the sound of Daniel's voice. Hadn't he said those very words the first time she had met him?

She stopped in her tracks and veered behind the checkout counter. Silly, but it afforded her a bit of security, a sense of separation.

His footsteps continued toward the gathering area. "Lilly?"

"I'm over here." She quickly flipped open the computer and acted busy, even as her face flamed. She was sure she wouldn't fool him for a moment, but she didn't know how else to handle facing him alone. No buffer like the teens or Jenna.

She sensed him standing across the counter. When he didn't say anything, she forced herself to look up.

He looked exhausted, with dark circles and beard

stubble, as if he'd been up for days. He stood there smiling—tentative, yet something in his eyes held… tenderness?

His expression ripped at her heart, causing further damage. She couldn't bear it. "Did you need something?"

"Yes." He swallowed. "I need to say I'm sorry."

Her heart went into a slow rhythm that sent blood whooshing in her ears.

"I really messed up. Because I've been afraid."

Dizziness made her sway. She gripped the countertop. "What?"

"I—" He took a step toward the end of the counter and stopped. "Can I come over there?" He thunked the countertop. "I really hate this thing."

She wasn't sure she could handle being so close. She needed to stay strong no matter his crazy talk. "We're fine where we are."

He gave a firm nod, jamming his hands in his pockets. The tender look was gone. Now Daniel looked outright scared. "It's hard to stay away from you when I have so much to say."

*Resist. Don't ask.* "Like what?" she blurted.

"Like the fact that, lately, I've let old hurts color my decisions for the future. I've made my own plans, living in my comfort zone, rather than truly depending on God for direction."

*Oh, my!* screeched through her mind, yet she

stood calmly, listening and waiting. *Could he be talking about his plan to move?*

"I haven't had much sleep the last few days. Have been thinking and praying. My dad and I talked, really talked. He showed me that I've been afraid of loving, of depending on others. No matter what I've told myself, I haven't trusted God's plan."

She managed an understanding nod. Her heart soared, because she thought she knew where this conversation might be going. But she didn't dare hope. Couldn't dare let feelings take over. She had to remain levelheaded. "So do you see God leading you another direction?"

*Oh, Lord, please let him say You've led him in* this *direction!*

The world's sweetest smile formed on his beautiful lips. Not the heart-stopping charmer smile. But a smile that warmed her to her toes. A smile that made her feel loved...cherished.

"Definitely another direction," he said. "The first direction is to the other side of this counter you're so good at using as a shield."

She bit back her own grin. "Can you blame me? I'll have you know this sales counter has served me nicely since that first night you came waltzing in here spouting off ideas about moving your church into the basement."

"You've been smart to protect yourself from me. But now I'm hoping we can both tear down the walls we've put up." He walked to the end of the counter but stopped, waiting for her invitation. "I think it's time for us to follow God's plan. Risky as it may seem to us."

Could she do it? Could she blow caution to the wind and step into a life she'd only dared dream of?

Jenna had stepped out in faith, claiming her happiness despite the fear. Maybe the time had come for Lilly to start dreaming again.

Surely she could, with God calling the shots.

Warmth infused her body, as if God Himself was pouring His love down on her, giving her courage.

She held out her hand, inviting Daniel.

He came to her and drew her into his arms. "I love you, Lilly."

She closed her eyes and breathed in his scent she'd missed so badly. "Oh, Daniel…I thought I'd never hear those words."

"I've spent the last several days talking with the church here and the one in Valdosta. I'm staying here in Corinthia. Please say you'll stay, too."

She pulled back far enough to look into his eyes—eyes that had grown so dear to her.

Overwhelming love, relief…and trepidation warred inside her.

"I sold a magazine article. I've been offered a position at a magazine in Louisville."

Concern filled his eyes. "I see."

"I don't want to give up on my dream career."

"You won't have to. You can do freelance work from home. Maybe hire someone to run the yarn shop. Would the magazine let you set up base here in Corinthia?"

How had she ever thought she could leave him? "I imagine I could make it work."

"I can't promise I won't make dumb mistakes or won't hurt you. But I can promise I'll do my best." He gently cupped her face in his large, capable hands. "Please don't leave me."

He said the last as if whispering a prayer.

She saw a lifetime of fear in his eyes. But he was making a commitment to her. To stay. To try.

That was all she could ask.

It was the least she could do, as well. "I'll stay." Joy burst through her. She threw her arms around his neck. "Yes! I'll stay. But I'll have to let our buyer know. We already signed an agreement."

He laughed as his lips closed in on hers.

All thoughts of business fled as his warm lips touched hers, tenderly, almost reverently.

Wrapped in his arms, she knew they could face anything as long as they were together.

## *Epilogue*

L illy walked in Frank's Pizza Place ready to do battle.

The representative for the investment company buying The Yarn Barn had informed the owners of the company that Lilly and Jenna wanted to back out of the deal, and apparently, one of the owners had refused, citing their signed agreement. The rep did say the owner might make a deal if she'd meet with him.

She figured the man didn't have a leg to stand on, but she didn't want the hassle of hiring a lawyer to handle it. So she had set up the appointment.

She planned to win him over…with pizza. She figured she could play hardball with the best of them, and trying to use a little of Daniel's charm couldn't hurt, either.

She'd armed herself in her best navy skirt and blazer. Crisp white blouse. Midheeled, business-like beige pumps. She walked into Frank's with purpose, briefcase in hand. Trying to look confident, prepared.

And there sat Daniel.

She glanced around the dining room, searching for a strange man in a suit.

"Oh, hey, Lilly," Frank called from beside the oven. "Daniel's at your regular table."

As much as she treasured those words, this wasn't the time. She gave Frank a quick wave and then hurried over to Daniel.

He'd been her rock the past few weeks. They'd been inseparable. She'd been happier than ever, except for this meeting hanging over her head.

She wanted this ordeal over. "I'm glad you came to support me, but I'd rather you leave. He's supposed to be here any minute."

"I *am* here."

She looked at him, confused. "Yes, of course you are. Now leave."

"Have a seat, Ms. Barnes. You're right on time for our meeting."

"Daniel, quit playing around. I have…" Mischief gleamed in his eyes making her forget what she was about to say. He was up to something. "What have you done? Did you contact the guy?"

He pulled out a chair for her. Once she was seated, he returned to his seat and leaned his arms on the table. "When you decided to sell and move away, I knew I had to do something. I figured you'd regret selling. And then what would you do when you realized you wanted to move back here to be near your family and friends?"

Shock made her spine snap up straight. "What are you saying?"

"I went to my dad for financial help. The two of us partnered to buy the shop in case you changed your mind."

She grabbed his hand. "Are you serious? You're the investment company?"

He nodded, a crooked, beautiful, *beloved* smile on his face.

After taking a few seconds to let the truth sink in, she burst out laughing. "I should be mad at you! I've been so stressed about this deal."

He gave her a smirk. "Well, I still have rights to buy it."

"You think you do, huh?"

"Although, I've been thinking...the shop would make the perfect wedding gift from me to you."

She held her breath as her stomach swooped to her feet.

He got up and came around the table. Went down on one knee.

"Daniel?" A nervous giggle escaped.

He presented a ring box with the most exquisite diamond ring she'd ever seen. It looked like an estate piece.

"Oh, my. Was that your mother's?"

Tears moistened his eyes. He nodded. "Lilly, I

love you and want to spend my life with you. Will you marry me?"

*Lord, thank You.*

She wanted to be his wife more than anything in the world. But she had to tease him a little, especially since he'd let her worry for the past few weeks. She put a saucy look on her face. "I don't know, Daniel. This seems a lot like a bribe to me."

Undeterred, he said, "I prefer to think of it as an incentive." He grinned at her, totally sure of himself. The charmer once again.

Laughter bubbled up and out from the deepest wounded part of her, a part that now felt healed and complete. Why torture him any more when she wanted this more than life itself? She wiggled the fingers of her left hand in front of him, demanding he put the ring on her. "Of course I'll marry you."

He slid the ring in place, then stood as he pulled her to her feet and gathered her in his arms. "I'm ready for a wedding as soon as you'll have me."

She knew she was ready, as well. To build their yarn shop business, their ministry and their life together.

\* \* \* \* \*

Dear Reader,

Thank you so much for hanging out with me again for this third story in the fictional town of Corinthia, Georgia! I hope you enjoyed Lilly and Daniel's journey to happiness.

Of course, both characters had a lot to learn about following God's plan for their lives. And don't we all tend to do that—either march ahead with our own foolish desires or cower in fear? God has had to remind me over and over again to trust in Him. It's not easy. But when we trust in His goodness, His mercy and His love for us, we can rest assured that we're on the right path. We're in capable hands!

Thank you so much for reading my book! I love hearing from readers. Please tell me what you think about *Georgia Sweethearts*. You can visit my website, www.missytippens.com, or email me at missytippens@aol.com. If you don't have internet access, you can write to me c/o Love Inspired Books, 233 Broadway, Suite 1001, New York, NY 10279.

*Missy Tippens*

## Questions for Discussion

1. At the beginning of the story, Lilly was trying to fulfill her aunt's wishes to run a yarn shop, even though she didn't know how to knit. How would you handle being asked to do a job you didn't feel qualified to do?

2. Daniel saw himself as having the gift to start new projects. What are some of your gifts or talents? How do you use them?

3. When Lilly and Daniel met, they felt an instant attraction. Do you believe in love at first sight? Why or why not?

4. Lilly and Daniel were both profoundly affected by childhood experiences. Can you give examples of ways those experiences affect us?

5. Daniel had a lot of tension with his father throughout the story. Who do you think was at fault?

6. Daniel served as a mentor for teen boys in the book. Who's been a mentor for you, and how has it affected your life?

7. The teenagers added another layer to the story. Did you think it added or detracted?

8. Lilly put her dream on hold to help raise her sister. Can you give examples of people you know who've sacrificed for family members?

9. Discuss the Bible verses listed at the beginning of the book. How do they apply to the story? How do they apply to your life?

10. At the end of the story, Daniel realizes he has mistaken his life's calling because of fear. Where do you think his fears stemmed from? Do you think that was realistic?

11. Do you know anyone like Vera from the story? How has that person affected your life, if at all? Do you think Vera is a happy person? Why or why not?

12. What do you think was the theme of this story?

13. What lessons did the main characters learn in this story?

14. Where's a place you like to hang out with friends, like the yarn shop in the book?

15. Do you have a person you know who is loving and supportive like Belinda? If so, share a little about that friend. If not, do you think you could be that person for someone else?

# LARGER-PRINT BOOKS!

## GET 2 FREE
## LARGER-PRINT NOVELS
## PLUS 2 FREE
## MYSTERY GIFTS

Love Inspired® SUSPENSE

RIVETING INSPIRATIONAL ROMANCE

### Larger-print novels are now available...

# *ReaderService*.com

## Manage your account online!
- Review your order history
- Manage your payments
- Update your address

*We've designed
the Harlequin® Reader Service
website just for you.*

## Enjoy all the features!
- Reader excerpts from any series
- Respond to mailings and special monthly offers
- Discover new series available to you
- Browse the Bonus Bucks catalog
- Share your feedback

*Visit us at:*
## ReaderService.com